Hardly Harding

Troy Bernardo

Troy Bernardo

Published by Jax and Maya Publishing

ISBN: 0-692-15175-3
ISBN-13: 978-0-692-15175-4

This novel is a work of fiction. Any reference to events, people, characters, products, establishments, or organizations are intended to give the fiction a sense of authenticity and reality or are a product of the author's imagination.

For Laura, Jax, and Maya

CONTENTS

Hardly Harding

PROLOGUE

The music cut out and I turned around to see that Jeff was putting a different CD in the player. He squinted at the back of his Styx: Greatest Hits album and started to flip through the tracks, looking back regularly at the numbers to ensure he didn't pass what song he was going for. He suddenly stopped, a grandiose smile on his face and flung the case in the stack next to the speakers. A light piano began and then the rest of the song picked up, filling the room with groans and confused faces as a few people recognized "Come Sail Away."

"Why does he always play this?" I asked Tim, "This is a house party. This is going to suck all the energy out of the room."

"He lives here too, Steve," Tim said calmly. "And he actually pays his rent on time."

"I told you, Tim, I'll pay you after the semester is over. My parents are pissed at me, and I just need some time to lay low and then ask them for money when Christmas break starts."

Tim rolled his eyes. His parents weren't helping him at all and he was figuring it out. Tuition, room, board, booze, weed, dates with different women, he was doing it all, and making A's in his classes while working a side job. Me on the other hand? I prided myself on always taking the path of least resistance, and somehow was still not even close to his level of success.

Jeff sauntered over, full of himself because of his song selection. A smile still across his face as he sang the lyrics as loud and drunkenly as he could.

"This is my shit!" He yelled over the music.

"Why?" I asked.

"How do you not like Styx?" Tim asked.

"It's not that I don't like Styx. It's nothing against the band. I'm just trying to throw a good party, and music like this, even if it's your, 'shit' Jeff, doesn't fit."

"Fuck you." Jeff replied, "When you pay your rent on time you can pick whatever song you want."

"Goddamnit! That has nothing to do with picking the song. It has to do with throwing a good party. Finals are over, I just want to get drunk and relax before I have to get back home and deal with my family."

Jeff mimed the drum solo, his long hair whipping around amid my yelling.

"Isn't your sister graduating from Yale or something?" Tim asked.

"You think my sister is graduating from law school in the middle of the year? It's winter break dude, turn your brain on. Also, stop asking about my sister."

Tim laughed while Jeff was still belting out half coherent lyrics from the song. I surveyed the room. It was a diverse group at the party. Tim was the kicker of the football team, so while we didn't get his A-list teammates, he did get some of the special team's guys to stop in. They were cool because we had a losing football team, and I often notice that losing teams seem to have more relaxed guys on it.

Jeff was the stoner who I don't think technically was supposed to be on campus anymore. He failed his nutrition class "Meet your Meat," and had been officially kicked out of school this semester because of a .5 GPA. His friends were smoking in the corner of the room wearing The Grateful Dead, The Doors, and Pink Floyd shirts. Then there was the mishmash of people we just invited over from our classes

"I'm going to go check on the keg," I told the boys as I headed to the back porch. We kept it there because it was an unseasonably warm night for Minnesota in December. When it was above freezing, we kept the keg outside so the beer stayed nice and cold. I gave the keg a lift and it felt about half full. I could hear the music stopped suddenly, and then the quiet piano intro music started again.

"Jeff restarted that damn song again," I said to myself. Now in no hurry to get back inside, I pumped the keg and started to fill up my empty cup. In the distance, I could hear sirens and myriad of other party sounds. Loud bass music thumping, drunk men yelling at each other, and sorority girls puking in backyards. It really did feel like the last day of the semester. One last hoorah before everyone goes back to their conservative parents, churches, and babysitting their little brothers and sisters.

I took out a cigarette, put it into my mouth and felt my pockets for a lighter, but I didn't feel the familiar protrusion.

"Can I have one of those?" I heard from behind me.

"Holy SHIT!" I yelled. I turned around to see a girl sitting on the edge of the porch. "How long have you been sitting there?"
"Like the whole time you've been getting a beer." She replied calmly.

The shadow from the overhang of our porch obscured her body and face, and unless you were really looking into the darkness, it was easy to assume she was just another shadow.

"Yeah, you can have one. You have a light?"

"Yeah, I got one." She said reaching into her pocket and pulling out a cheap lighter. I traded it for a cigarette and lit mine. Then I reached over and lit hers as well. The flame only flickered, but for a brief second, I saw her face. She had light blonde hair, soft green eyes which, for whatever reason, I wasn't expecting. When she took her first drag, she didn't look at the end of the cigarette, just at me. A smile crept up her face as the flame went out and I saw the smoke billow out of her mouth.

"Thanks." She said.

"How did you find out about the party?" I asked.

"It's the last day of finals. There are always parties. I just walk around from one to the next seeing what is going on." "You just crash a bunch of strangers' parties?"

"Yeah. I'm a small, white girl, I can walk into whatever party I want."

"You can't argue with that logic."

"Truthfully, you would be able to do the same. A dark-haired, slim, white guy doesn't arouse a lot of suspicion."

"So how many parties have you been to tonight?" I asked.

"Tonight? About six? Maybe eight?"

"How does this one stack up?"

"I don't know yet, I haven't even been inside."

"Well, I don't mean to brag, but we have some of the football players here."

"Real life football players from our winless team?! Who is here?"

"The kicker and some other bench guys. Some of them might actually go pro."

"Really?"

"No. Of course not."

We both laughed and took a drag from our cigarettes.

"You know, we can smoke inside if you want."

"This must be a fancy party." She said flatly.

"Do you want the free smokes and beer or not?"

I could tell it was a tempting offer, even if she was crashing different parties. Eventually, you have to settle down and actually stay at one because people would start to recognize a new face showing up as the night was winding down.

"Fine. I'll do it for the beer. I'm Linda," she said abruptly.

"I'm Steve."

Troy Bernardo

FALL

1

"And how does that make you feel?" Rachel asked, without looking up from her notepad.

"Not very good, Rachel." I replied.

"Do you want to elaborate on that?" She said jotting something down.

"Not really."

Rachel let out a heavy sigh and continued to write frantically without any meaningful system. She didn't care. I didn't care. Nobody really cared. It doesn't take a medical degree to see that, and Dr. Rachel, who strongly advised we go on a first name basis, knew I was getting nothing from the sessions. She just kept up the charade as long as I kept paying the bill, and I kept going for the illusion that I was continuing to work on myself for Linda. It was a delicate and pointless dance. Generally, Linda and I did these sessions together, but Dr. Rachel thought it would be beneficial for us to split the hour and spend one on one time with her.

"I'm going to be honest with you, Steven." Dr. Rachel asserted. She had finally stopped writing and had a distant look in her eyes as she was speaking to me. She sat across the room in a deep, leather chair, but she might as well have been clocked out and driving home considering what takeout she wanted to order for dinner. Hell, I might as well not be there at all. She could do this to an empty room. Her interest, compassion, advice, it was all empty. It was a stranger trying to piece together one of the most complex and meaningful relationships two people can have. Rachel had no emotional attachment to Linda and I. The only time I had seen a rise out of her was when the co-pay wasn't going through because of an insurance complication.

"I think you and Linda have a great chance of putting it all back together and moving on with your lives. Just remember my advice. Try to enjoy one another again. Just go out on a date after this is done." She said this curtly and then hastily looked down at her notebook.

"What do you think that will do?"

"What?"

"The date? Why? We see each other all the time, why would this help?"

She stopped writing again and sighed heavily. Then looked at her watch.

"Time's up."

2

Dr. Rachel's office was in a big, nondescript concrete building, and although I never checked, I seriously doubt the only business in there was therapy. It looked like the kind of structure that has several call centers cycling in and out of it every few months. I had the second of the two sessions, and as I walked outside, I started to scan the streets for Linda. Immediately the hot, muggy Minneapolis heat bore down on me. I never understood how the summers in this state could be so overbearing and the winters so unbearable.

I saw Linda sitting on a bench under a tree. She was going through her phone and checking her emails. After a minute of waiting for her to say something, and nothing happening, I broke the silence.

"Dr. Rachel recommended we go out on a date tonight. Maybe it would be fun to try a new restaurant? I think Groupon has a few new places on it we have been meaning to try."

"How about The Lowry?" Linda replied as she stood up, still looking at her phone.

"I just thought it would be fun to try a new place." This statement wasn't ignored, but it certainly wasn't considered.

"Let's just go to The Lowry. It's almost like our tradition now."

She didn't wait for a response. She just turned around and started walking the half a block up toward her favorite post-therapy restaurant. It's not that The Lowry has lousy food, or the convenience of it being kitty-corner from Dr. Rachel are the problems. The issue I have with it is we go there every Wednesday night after we have therapy. We go and sit down in the same booth, with the same waitress, order the same drinks, and get the same food.

Of course, I didn't say this. When I disrupt the routine Linda gets upset because she has a system in place of drinking half of my beer and then eating half of my food. Essentially, when we go to The Lowry, Linda orders half of everything so she can have the consistency she craves while having a variety she wants.

Most of my interactions, with Linda or any person, follows a simple equation. My desired outcome, minus the energy that is taken arguing that outcome, needs to be greater than it being worth it. With Linda, it generally was never worth the effort of arguing.

We walked into The Lowry which itself is a strange looking restaurant. It's painted a dark blue, and individual light bulbs light up the letters of its name. It's supposed to be minimalist because their sign states, "Burgers Whiskey Oysters Eggs," with no punctuation. It's like if the Apple store tried to open a restaurant, but then realized they didn't know what they were doing, panicked and just hired some overqualified Denny's cook. The place felt stuck between two worlds. It wanted to be chic so badly, but the decorations tried too hard to make it that way. All that attempt at originality fell into a banality of blandness. It was working so hard to be original that it wasn't anything but ordinary.

The best example of this is the fact that there is no diversity in the wait staff. When I say, "diversity," I don't mean black and white people, I mean just any difference in the people. All the employees had a facial piercing. For girls, they all had a nose ring and for boys an eyebrow stud. Every one of them had visible tattoos on their hands, or forearm, or both, and most had a funky, alternative hairstyle. I'm not saying these people didn't have personality, or their own viewpoints or even their own life experiences, but when you put them all into one place like this, it devalues why they do all of the things they do to stand out. In The Lowry, every single individual is just another boring person.

None of them are unique because all of them are.

Wanda, our usual waitress, started toward our table with menus in her hands. She had a new tattoo of a pin-up girl that was scabbing over on her forearm. It was a unique choice and I really only saw a tattoo like hers on old sailors in movies. Still, it wasn't going to be enough to stand out. Once she realized who we were, she just nodded, "The usual?" She asked. She didn't even wait for a response or stop walking, as she went right back into the kitchen.

Linda then went on her phone. She sent a few texts and played Dining Dash for a few minutes. This was followed by reading the latest Yelp reviews on The Lowry and commenting on the patrons who left the restaurant one star.

"How was your session with Dr. Rachel?" I asked to break Linda's commenting on the comments.

"Good!" She replied enthusiastically. "You know, she's the best in the business."

"Business of what?" I asked.

Linda glared at me. The faint light from her phone revealing the quick frustration she had with my question.

"The business of saving marriages," she replied snidely.

"It's strange to me that's considered a business."

"Everything is a business," Linda countered as she looked back into her phone. Wanda showed up at our table and put down one Saison and an IPA from Surly Brewing.

"The turkey burger was dry and unseasoned?" Linda said indignantly, "How could someone even think that?"

I looked at Linda. She didn't have anything more to say. I could have pushed back and come up with times she complained about the turkey burger, but how could I possibly win in this argument? I smiled at her, but she was lost in a world of peer reviews and likes. I looked down into my beer, sighed, and took a drink. The fizz and bubbles making nameless, shapeless figures that quickly drifted from the middle of the glass to the edge and dissipated.

Linda gasped from across the table, and I looked up.

"Emily got engaged! There's a picture of her ring on Facebook!"

She flipped her phone around to show me the picture of an engagement ring that looked the same as everyone else's.

3

"Thursday is my least favorite day of the week," the elderly woman next to me said feebly as she was sitting down.

"I agree," I replied, forcing a smile while putting my headphones back into my ears. The old woman started to pout. I didn't want to be rude, but I tried my best to ignore her because this was the only time I get to relax. The buses to and from work are the rare moments when I get to zone out and spend time doing what I like to do. Some people prefer to read, listen to podcasts or music, or talk to their neighbor on the bus. Generally, only the older people prefer the latter option. Personally, I enjoy sitting on the bus with earphones in with absolutely nothing on.

It would be great to spend the time without the headphones in, but when they aren't in, people start to talk to you. This initially wasn't something I worried about until roughly eight months ago when a man wearing a Jacksonville Jaguars jersey asked me extraordinarily uncomfortable personal questions and proceeded to chug 40-ounces of Miller High Life. This would have been less alarming if somebody on the bus had noticed or cared. It was also troubling because it was 6:30 in the morning on a Tuesday.

I have tried a few times to listen to podcasts and classical music. I have tried reading and even pretending to read on the bus. I just can't get the same blank feeling I get from absolutely no distraction. For those twenty-three minutes on the bus, twenty-eight if there's some traffic, thirty-two if there's fresh snow, close to forty-two if there's traffic and snow, I get to be free. Free of Linda, my job, Facebook friends I haven't spoken to since high school, my apartment, and I get true peace. Nobody is going to take that away from me. Especially not a lonely old woman.

We stopped again and picked up a variety of about ten people. Four were middle-aged professionals heading downtown for another day of work. They all had the same defeated look on their faces. Three were young college students. I could tell because of their backpacks, youthful carelessness, and overall unemployable demeanor. Two looked like blue-collar workers from their sun-beaten faces and leathery skin. The last one was a drunk homeless man.

I always wondered why homeless people use the bus so much. The one advantage a homeless man has over me is that he has no responsibilities. Why use any of the small amount of money you have on a bus ticket? There's no rush. This guy didn't have an important client to see this morning. He doesn't need to pick up bagels for the office. That's $2.25 you wasted getting downtown that you could have spent on food or alcohol. Then again, I'm sure some of the reason this guy was homeless was that he lacked forward thinking abilities.

4

"You're late," Jim said sternly.

"Sorry," I replied, "there was a lot of traffic on the road this morning."

Jim shifted his coffee mug from one hand to the other with a disappointed scowl on his face and turned his wrist toward his eyes so he could pretend to look at the time on his watch. This gave me a chance to notice the big bold letters on his mug that said **CLEVELAND**, with the skyline of the city in the background. "You know," he started to slowly look up from his watch and dragged his eyes across the vertical lines on my shirt. "Veronica lives in your neighborhood, and she was here at 8:55."

I was already walking away to my office by the time he finished his sentence. I got my keys out of my pocket, unlocked the door, turned on the lights, and drew the blinds so nobody could see me. I logged into my computer, and the time on my desktop read 9:04. While technically Jim was right about being late, there certainly wasn't anything he could do about such a small, meaningless infraction. Yes, Jim was my boss, and yes, I would routinely show up five to ten minutes late. However, I did marry Jim's boss's, boss's, boss's daughter. While a career in middle management in health insurance didn't seem like what I drew up as a child, few things often do.

The most important thing to do daily for any office job is to show up on time, if not a little early. Over half of the job is being on time, and if you aren't married to the boss's daughter, this can propel your career all the way to a sweet, sweet $42,000 annual salary you've been dreaming of. All of this just after wasting three to five years of your life. The second most important thing to do is just look busy. Book unnecessary meetings, be on the phone even if you aren't talking to anyone, make a few PowerPoint presentations and make sure everyone thinks that you know more than you do. Make yourself seem invaluable.

What I never understood about corporate America and companies like this one is it seems like a shell of a place that wants to make money. If you're going to be a successful business or even a moderately successful business, you should try and reduce expenses and increase profits. While we cut costs in some areas like equipment, health insurance, and paying the employees we have livable wages, we also just say we need to reduce these costs so the bosses can make more money, and we can hire more employees who do less work. Veronica, the stellar employee who shows up at 8:55 every day, spends her day looking up cat videos on her computer. Now, I'm not saying I don't waste time at work, but if the big differentiator between the two of us is nine minutes, then I don't think we're digging deep enough.

On the bright side, it was only three hours until lunch.

5

"You're not going to go all *Fight Club* on me, are you?" John asked grinning through his unkempt beard.

"I don't know what you mean, John," I replied as I took another swig of my beer. John had a habit of trying to be clever, but it never worked. He wasn't dumb, I just often didn't know what he was talking about.

"You've never seen the film or read the book *Fight Club*?" He said in an exhausted tone.

"I've seen the movie, I just don't see how that relates."

"You just seem like you might go postal any second."

"It's not like that." I took a pill bottle out of my pocket and shuffled two into my palm.

"How's the new medication going?"

"Not great."

"Does the doctor recommend you mix it with alcohol?"

"Funny," I sneered as I washed them down with a skunky happy hour beer.

"I tried those for a while you know," John said in a serious tone, "They left me feeling anxious and empty."

"I haven't told you what I'm taking."

"All anti-anxiety meds are the same."

John propped his arms up on the table and leaned the side of his face into his palm. He was an interesting character. After working in the food industry for nearly ten years, he left it for an entry-level job at my company. We started at the same time and were in the same training class; however, I ascended in the ranks faster than he did because of whom my wife was. After about three years, I had an office, and John was still in his introductory, on the phone role in insurance sales. Upper management sells it to him as, "good experience." We continued to meet weekly for a beer.

"I don't want you to take this the wrong way," John nearly whispered in a somber tone. "I want to know why you're taking those pills."

"Because I have anxiety."

"About what though? I mean, you have a good wife even if things aren't perfect, you have friends, and your father-in-law would never let you get fired for any small bullshit, so what are you nervous about?"

"Let me ask you something," I also nearly whispered in a mocking tone. "Why did you take anti-anxiety pills?"

"Oh, that's easy! I was a complete wreck when I took those pills, and they're an easy fix. I realized I needed to make significant changes in my life to be happy so I did. I quit my job, dumped my long-term girlfriend, and started a career with significantly less stress."

"How did you motivate yourself to do all that?"

"I don't know. I guess I just didn't want to be miserable anymore. I mean, when push comes to shove, my problems are minuscule compared to real world shit going on outside of the U.S. I've never been a sex slave or a child soldier. I think all my issues were kind of petty looking back at them."

John moved his hands from his cheek and laid his palms face-up on the thick wood table, giving me a glance at the numerous, bulbous cysts that lined up and down his arm. I wondered why he never got them removed. I wondered if he cared that they somewhat deformed the tattoos that were on his forearms.

"I struggled with depression and anxiety for a long time Steven," he said after a few moments of silence. "I know you aren't supposed to say this to someone struggling with mental health, but stop being such a pussy dude."

"What the fuck, John?"

"I'm just being a dick, Steve. But I don't understand where these issues are coming from."

"It's hard to describe."

"Can you at least try?"

"I don't know. I just feel empty."

"Well, depression and anxiety can manifest itself in different ways for different people. I'm just saying if I had your life, I wouldn't be so quick to complain about it."

"Well, that's not really fair for you to say."

"Steve, the reason I struggled with depression was because of my shitty job in food production where I worked ten hour days with people on various drugs. Then I would go home to a girlfriend who was depressed and not working and living off me. In addition to all that, my boss was a bastard. I'm just saying your situation is a little different."

"Did you start taking those pills to cope with how small your dick is?"

John sighed and shook his head. He looked into his beer and spaced out for a minute. I could tell he wasn't sure how to deal with the situation. On the one hand, I was a friend who needed help, and he was someone who was experienced in this world of mental health issues and various medications. He had the background to help me figure out the next steps and not make rash decisions. On the other hand, I was being an asshole.

"I just want to help you, man." John said almost pleading with me, "Please just try to snap out of whatever this is."

"I'll try. Honestly, I don't know what my other options are."

"Steven?" I heard a surprised voice behind me mutter. "Steven Harding?"

At first, I figured it was our waitress, but as I turned my head, I saw a heavyset woman about my age. Her eyes were wide, and she had a smile plastered on her face. She also had her arms out toward me, ready for a hug. I didn't recognize her at all. I quickly went through the long list of places I could potentially know her from. Social groups like the country club, book club, wine tastings, all turned up nothing. I then thought of college, one-night stands, girls at bars, friends, girlfriends, friends' girlfriends, chicks I made out with in high school, but still couldn't come up with any memory.

"You don't recognize me?" She said in a disappointed tone.

"I'm sorry," I replied with a frown.

John laughed in the background.

"It's me! Marcy Broomshankle!"

That name meant nothing to me.

"Oh my goodness, Marcy! You look so different," I blurted out instinctively. I went in and hugged her, and the smile lit up her face again. "God, I can't even remember the last time I saw you," I said hoping I could get a clue as to who she was.

"It's been too long," she said without hesitation. "I married Dan Geitsfeld a few years ago, and we have two kids."

"How is Dan doing?" I inquired hoping to get some sort of clue.

"He's doing well. He's still working at the mill outside of town. He's the manager now, so that's good."

A brief silence hung in the air. An uncomfortable feeling that this interaction would never end. My mind frantically raced as to who this woman was and who Dan was. If she hadn't known my name, I would have guaranteed she had the wrong person. I've never known anyone who worked at the mill. I didn't even know what the mill was.

"How old are your kids?" I asked to break the tension.

Marcy took her phone out of her pocket and opened up her pictures. The kids were Hitler's dream. Snowy white skin, blonde hair, and blue eyes. Real WASPy looking. She said gleefully, "Mark is three, but Anna is turning five this Saturday. We're throwing a low-key BBQ party for her. We have a bouncy house and a horse coming for the kids. The adults are having a keg and a case of wine inside." Her eyes widened at me, and she said joyously, "You should come!"

I have a general rule that I deny such invitations. I never know how drunk I can get at gatherings like this one and I never seem to be able to be the right amount. I can be too sober to deal with kids, or too drunk to be around them. I never hit that sweet spot. Something about Marcy made me want to go though. Not because she had a warmth about her, or because she seemed sincere about me coming, but because I was so genuinely intrigued about who this person was.

"I would have to clear it with my wife," I said with a smile. "But that sounds lovely."

"Great!" She replied, "I'll Facebook you all the details later tonight!" Just like that she turned around and started to wander out the door. When she made it to the exit she turned around and said full of sincerity, "It was good seeing you again."

"You as well, Marcy."

She smiled one last time and continued walking away.

The door opened, and hot air rushed into the bar. I sat back down, and John sighed. "Who was that?" He asked after a few seconds.

"Marcy?" I replied, finishing off my beer.

"She looks like she was really hot back in the day. You know, before the kids."

"Maybe."

"How do you just forget people like that?" John said with concern in his voice, "I feel like every fifth time we're in here someone comes up to you to just say 'hello' and you never know who any of them are."

"Can I have another one?" I asked the waitress as she walked by.

"Just try and get involved in what's going around you a little bit. I bet if you had networked even twenty percent of the total contacts you've made in your life, you wouldn't have to work for your wife's dad."

The waitress came by and dropped off another beer.

"I already had it poured. It's on the house." She said not stopping and went across the bar to get more orders.

"See, John! Sometimes good things just happen." I said picking up the beer.

John rolled his eyes.

"Are you going to the birthday party at least?" He asked. "You might be able to meet someone in a startup or something. Get out of your cush job it's almost impossible to get fired, and trade it out for a new stressful one."

"I'm not going," I replied. I know he was just trying to help, but he wasn't.

"Then why would you say you'd go?" John asked.

"I really just wanted the whole conversation to be over. I hate it when I get stuck in situations like that one."

"That situation was 100% your fault."

"Even if that were true, who invites essentially a stranger to their child's birthday party?"

"Someone who was excited to see you, Steve."

"I doubt that," I said, taking another gulp of my beer.

6

I stumbled into the apartment at about 9:30. It wasn't that it was too late to come home. The problem was John and I started drinking right when we got out of work. Not casual, sexy drinking either. We weren't two guys from *Mad Men* sharing a few after work whiskeys. This was sloppy, frustrated, angry drinking that if done too often can make people question if you're mentally stable. Linda was sitting on the couch, drinking a glass of wine and staring at the TV. The Real Housewives of something emanated a soft glow, and I heard several loud beeps cover up the colorful language. Linda looked at the gaudy clock that hung on an otherwise bare wall to the right of her. She sighed and poured another glass of wine. From the faint light, I could tell the bottle was more than 75% empty.

"How's John?" She asked.

"Good," I replied.

"You guys drink a lot?"

"Some."

"How many is 'some'?" She mocked.

"Just some."

I made my way into the kitchen and opened up the fridge. I pulled a beer out and used the wooden counter as a wedge to pop the bottle cap off. The loud *THUD* echoed in the apartment, and Linda yelled, "Don't do that. You're destroying the edge of the island."

I ran my fingers along the chewed up wood. Every time I did this Linda told me to stop, and every time I did it. I wouldn't say I did it to be defiant, I considered this more of a convenience. The bottle opener was always in a new spot in the kitchen, and unless I immediately opened my drink, I was in danger of being told I had already drunk enough for the evening and I needed to switch to water.

I walked into the living room and saw Linda's wine glass was already half empty and she was rapidly finishing the bottom half. Before I sat down, she motioned back to the door. She swallowed the wine and blurted out, "Don't forget about Drew and Amanda's wedding next month."

"Why are you pointing at the door?"

"I'm not pointing at the door, I'm pointing at cork board." She tried to accentuate this by pointing harder.

I turned and saw there was a small cork board on the wall at about eye level. On it were a few little things. A receipt from some shoe store, two save the dates and three wedding invitations. I found the board itself off-putting because it was a shade of white that almost blended into the wall. I took a sip of the beer and went to go sit down next to Linda.

"I figured we could write some nice notes on it to each other or something," she said.

"Yeah, maybe."

"You don't like it?"

I shrugged my shoulders.

"Well, it will at least keep us more organized."

With that, Linda finished off her glass of wine and poured another. This time the entire bottle was turned over and every last drop quietly splashed into her glass. A few minutes of silence passed.

"What's the point of this show?" I asked as two women were arguing on a yacht.

"There isn't a point," Linda replied, distracted by the argument.

"Then why watch it?"

"I'm just trying to relax, Steve. This is relaxing."

"These women are screaming at each other and getting into fistfights. How is this relaxing?"

Linda didn't answer. She just sat there, entranced by two women she would never talk to in real life having a staged argument.

7

John and I should have finished closer to 7:00 than 9:00 last night, and I could feel it. As the elevator doors opened, Jim was leaning against the wall across from me. He had a coffee cup in one hand and was militantly staring at his watch.

"Good morning Steven," Jim exclaimed through a big smile without looking up.

I grunted as I made my way past him and walked toward my office. Jim could tell when I was hungover, and even though he was technically my boss, he still knew better than to ask any questions when I felt this rocky. It's not that I was particularly disheveled on days like this, or that I was more tired than usual. It was just that I gave off more of a toxic, disagreeable vibe that people can sense just from looking at me. That, in addition to the fact that after a night of boozing, I tend to have a vinegary aroma from sweating out the alcohol gives off a negative aura. Still, Jim would act cheerful, because he knew it made me angry.

I opened my office door and walked behind my desk. I sat down and started digging through my drawers to find eye drops and get some ibuprofen for my headache. I had picked up my phone and placed it against my ear to call John to see how he was doing when suddenly my door burst open and Veronica was standing there, nearly out of breath and tomato faced. She was mad, but even if you liked Veronica, she's not a woman you can ever take seriously. She's a Midwestern woman through and through. Obese and there isn't anything she is ever going to do about it. Her milky white skin with dark hair contrasted nicely, and if it weren't for the additional 100 pounds she was packing she really wouldn't be a bad looking lady.

"This isn't the right form," Veronica said sternly and loudly. "This is the *green* AR-735." She stopped for a second and stared at me, bewildered because of my lack of response. She continued to wheeze and finally said, "For our handling team to continue, as is the procedure, we need you to submit the *yellow* AR-735 form. If you don't, it delays the whole process by at least 24 hours! We lose an entire business day to get this completed." Her eyes narrowed, her brow furrowed, and her lips tightened.

She didn't even give me enough time to hang up the phone. Now, had I actually cared about my job I could call HR, and fill out a form because this was a clear case of insubordination. This, in turn, would result in a formal strike against her record, and if she got too many of these it could prevent her from being promoted and potentially she could be fired. Also, she would probably need to take an online class and have a few face-to-face meetings with some senior HR representative to make sure that she understood the hierarchy of an office.

However, nobody actually respects anyone who fills out complaints. Continual slaps on the wrists and meetings just make the whistleblower look like a Grade A pushover. That's when an idea sprung into my head to deal with this problem and insure that I would be able to nap the rest of the day undisturbed.

"Yes, Mr. Richardson," I pretend to reply, sternly holding up a finger to Veronica. Her face continued to contort as her frustration grew. "I apologize for all of that noise, it was just an overzealous salesperson." I uncomfortably laughed, waited for a few beats, and gave a solemn grunt. "I assure you, I have my office under control. Genera-."

Now, *my* eyes sharply moved to Veronica's, and *my* lips tightened. "Well, if you change your mind, please feel free to give me a call." I hung up the phone and sat in a heavy silence.

"Like I was saying," Veronica immediately started again. Like what I was doing wasn't important. Like her time was more valuable than mine.

"Veronica," I interrupted, "do you know who was just on the phone there?"

"That doesn't matter, this is-"

"That was Mr. Richardson. He is a relatively small business owner in the suburbs who was trying to work out a health insurance deal for his twenty-five employees."

Veronica stared at me like I was painting she couldn't understand. Nothing was going on behind those eyes. She had no clue what was happening.

"Do you want to know why he won't be getting insurance with us now?" I paused to give her a chance to guess, but she continued to give me that deer in a headlights stare. "It's because of you!" I snapped. I saw chairs swivel and heads pop up over their cubicle walls. "You alone have cost this company tens of thousands of dollars because of an order for extra sheets of paper for the printer because that is all the AR-735 forms do. I understand that your biggest contribution to this company is the paper being stocked weeks in advance in my copy room, but I am actually trying to pump some money into this place, so we don't need to lay off employees like you"

I was digging deep. I generally am not the kind of person to throw things around like that in the office, but the combination of the lecture yesterday from Jim, the way she spoke to me, mixed with the hangover really pushed me over the edge.

"Now," I said in almost a whisper, "get out of my office."

Her eyes had now welled up with tears, and she made her way back to her desk. Slowly I saw heads go back down in their cubicles and once everyone was sitting down and facing their computer, I knew it was safe to close the blinds to my office and shut the door. I turned off the lights and laid down on my couch.

I knew the difference in the stupid goddamn forms. I knew that they preferred yellow to green cover sheets. This was all day one training bullshit. This is how I kept my job. I would make a few small mistakes, wait for someone to jump out of line, pretend like it was during a very inopportune time, and level them. This made me look competent and downplay others' importance in the office. A display like that could set a strong tone for six months. Especially to a waste of space like Veronica. I guarantee you, after a spectacle lie that nobody would be late for two weeks, and nobody would come bursting into my office telling me how to do a meaningless paper request form.

"Believe it or not, it takes a lot of thought to be lazy," I thought as I dry-heaved into my trashcan.

8

"How's your job going, Steven?" Mom asked with a bit of genuine sincerity.

"It's fine," I lied without even looking up from my plate.

"When I was your age Steve, I already had started Globonet," Dad bragged.

"That's great, Dad," I replied through a mouthful of ham steak.

"How about your job, Abby?" Mom asked my sister.

Abby rolled her eyes deep into her skull. She did this a lot as a humble way to brag about something without it seeming like she actually wanted to. This was a loophole she commonly exploited in an attempt to sell you that her life was indeed, much better than yours while seeming apprehensive to do so. While I am sure nobody envies my life, my sister's life isn't one I would trade for.

"The firm I'm at now is really, really jerking me around," she started, firmly putting her fork down next to her plate. This was a telltale sign that this was going to be a long brag. "They fired my mentor because she tried to stand up for herself and not just pass the buck to someone else." Abby, realizing that she wasn't doing anything now at dinner other than talk, self-consciously spooned some extra green beans onto her plate.

"That's just terrible management," Dad commentated, shaking his head in disapproval. "That behavior never would have gone on at my company."

"So," my sister started again, "I start poking around and seeing if I can get any offers from other firms. Eventually, this headhunter approaches me and tells me she can get me a job at a rival firm with a pay bump and a nice bonus."

Almost nobody was listening at this point. My father was already lost in thinking about how much more superior his company was than this firm. My mother was worried because not many people were eating the ham steak. Linda hadn't said a word since we greeted my parents three hours ago. My brother was stoned. To top it all off, I was busy shoveling ham into my mouth as Linda could not cook at all, and this was my first decent meal in a week. The only reason I drive out to the suburbs every Sunday for family dinner, a tradition I have upheld since college, is because I rarely get to eat a home cooked meal anymore. It's all take-out and frozen food you put in the oven. My Mom can't cook well, but compared to Linda, her food was actually edible.

"You know," my Dad started suddenly, "I have always wondered why elephants liked peanuts. It can't be that they found them in Africa when they were in the wild, right? I remember when I was a kid and the circus came to town. I was standing ten feet away from an elephant, and I saw him pick up the peanuts with his trunk, put them in his mouth and shell them. I always wondered how they learned that."

"It's a 50,000 dollar bonus!" My sister exclaimed, once again rolling her eyes. Trying to sell us that number wasn't built into her self-worth.

My brother, Sergio, got up and walked to the sink. He cleaned off his plate and headed into his room with no visible reaction on his face. Nobody addressed this. Unfortunately for him the economy just wasn't conducive to a psychology and history major with a minor in world religions. Being twenty-four and intelligent and being forced to live at home and listen to this every Sunday tested him.

Personally, I really don't like it when people complain about their families because I have seen some bad ones. One of my best friends, Victor, had his father die in a motorcycle accident when he was five. Then when we were in college, his step-dad committed suicide in front of his mom. This wasn't even a, "bad," family in the conventional sense, just an unlucky one. You could have drug addicted, abusive, jobless, moneyless, homeless, or drunk families. None of us were in jail. All of us had somewhere to live. None of us had an affinity for heroin. But is that really the mark we should measure it against? The absolute rock bottom? Should I consider my marriage a success just because Linda and I weren't split up?

"You know, sometimes when I see snakes slithering in the grass, I wonder if they can feel the difference between it and water," Dad started again. "Like Water Moccasins. Can they feel the difference? Or can they feel a different sensation?"

"How's your job going, Steven?" Mom interrupted to stop Dad's strange animal ravings.

"It's fine," I told her again.

Nobody even noticed that she had asked this before and I had now answered the question twice in ten minutes. Then we sat there for a while. Nobody said anything, and we all were just moving food around our plates desperately searching for something to say.

9

Linda had a broad smile on her face as I closed the door behind me. It was the first big smile I had seen in a long time. Lately, her face was one of frustration. Not necessarily because of me, but I don't think I was helping. I put my bag down next to the door and saw she was drinking a glass of red wine, the bottle only half empty.

"What are you so happy about?" I asked. "Usually you wait until dinner to crack open the wine."

Linda didn't respond right away, but her smile did go down noticeably. After a few seconds, she said in a matter of fact tone, "I bought something today."

"Was it expensive? With a face like that, I feel like it is going to be expensive."

"It was only about one-hundred dollars."

"That's not bad at all." I wandered into the kitchen and got myself a glass from the cupboard.

"Careful!" she exclaimed, as I turned away from the glasses.

I looked down at the ground and thoroughly examined my surroundings. Nothing was on the floor other than a few old plastic water bottles and one of my socks that I forgot to put into the hamper. I was about to ask her what I should be careful about when I heard a faint jingle coming from another room. Initially, I thought I was hearing things. After a few seconds of standing perfectly still I heard it again, only this time it was more of a sustained light ringing.

Out from my study, a kitten popped his head around the corner and looked at me suspiciously. He was a relatively older kitten. His fur was a mid-length, and the color was a light orange. He had piercing green eyes that were quickly being consumed by his growing pupils. He then made a dash for Linda, who picked him up and stroked him on the back.

"His name is Jackson," she said calmly, a soft purr radiated from his tiny body.

I walked through the kitchen and into the study. I saw that the place had been converted into Jackson's room. The floor was covered with cat toys, strings, and catnip and the corner of the room now had a litter box that was surrounded with loose litter.

"What the hell?" Was the only thing I was able to finally utter.

"Steve, Jackson needed a home, and we are lucky enough to have an empty one. He was at a kill shelter, and in two days he was going to be put down. Have some compassion for him." Her face softened as his purrs became more audible.

"Linda, I'm allergic to cats. You know that. Why do you think it would be appropriate to do any of this?"

Linda looked up from Jackson and stared coldly at me. She put him down onto the ground and let him scamper back into what was now his room, all the while a soft jingle from the bell on his collar let me know where he was without turning my head. Her eyes narrowed, and her nostrils flared.

"Fine," she blurted out stomping a foot on the floor, "I won't make you keep him."

I let out a sigh of relief, "Thank you." I replied.

"However, I will not have a hand in this poor kitten's death. If you want to get rid of him, you will need to take him back to the Humane Society yourself."

"Do you have any idea how fucked up that is?"

"I don't care."

She turned around, stormed out of the kitchen and marched down the hallway. After a few seconds, I could hear the bedroom door slam so hard that it echoed in the apartment. I turned around and faced the entrance to my study that now had a cat sitting in the doorway.

I didn't panic. She did this sometimes. She grew up in an environment that didn't discipline, and this is what happens when there is no structure in a home. Parents think their kids grow out of the attitude, but I can tell you full of confidence Linda hadn't. This would be the same scene if she found a kitten on the side of the road and was ten years old.

I filled the wine glass up, pouring it heavy. This wasn't something I was going to take lightly, and I wasn't going to think about it sober. I downed half the glass and grimaced as I pivoted toward the cat. He perked up and meowed almost inaudibly at me. In that moment while I was staring at Jackson, I really began to consider my two options and weigh which one of them would be best. While I cannot live with a cat or a dog because of my allergies, the fact that I would personally be condemning one to death was something I didn't expect to do after work that day. I would be lying if I said the images didn't start popping into my head. I began to think about Jackson being led down a sterile hallway to be euthanized by some vet who didn't have the ability to be a real vet and open his own practice. Instead, he just kills animals because he drank too much during veterinary school. That thought made my stomach turn, and I could feel the fear and confusion Jackson would experience being brought back to the pound after living in a home for a day.

On the other hand, staying near any kind of cat for a prolonged period of time results in my eyes watering and swelling up so severely that I can hardly see. Jackson left the open doorway to his room and softly pranced to my feet. He let out another squeak that was supposed to be a meow, and he looked up at me with a confused but happy glint in his soft green eyes. I picked him up and held him close to my chest. The warmth of my body made him happy, and he purred as he closed his eyes. After a few minutes, my eyes started to water and snot ran down my nose onto my upper lip.

"Steve?" I heard softly from behind me.

I turned around and saw Linda staring at me from down the darkened hallway with a loving grin. She ran toward me and gave me a hug as she started to cry. What was initially just a few tears turned into sobbing, and she really let go of some deeply pent-up emotions as she wept into my shirt.

Once she had calmed down, she whispered, "I'm so glad you changed your mind." She looked up at me, eyes beaming, proud of my sacrifice and grabbed Jackson from my arms and brought him into the bedroom.

I stood there in the kitchen for a while just drinking huge gulps of wine and then refilling it and drinking more until my mouth felt dry and my stomach started to turn from the warm, thick booze that was coating my insides. My shirt stuck to my chest where Linda's hot, salty tears had soaked through. Even after all that, I still didn't have the heart to tell her that I had an allergic reaction and I already decided to take him back to the Humane Society.

10

The cool air whipped my face and chapped my lips. It wasn't winter yet, but the cold snap, while we transitioned out of fall, was a reminder of the harsh months that were about to come. The worst part of winter is driving, but luckily my commute and jaunts around town were nearly all with the help of public transit.

When the bus pulled up, I hastily got on and started to move toward the back. Most of the seats were empty, and nobody was sitting together at this point. Almost all the passengers were seated next to the window, allowing a passenger to sit in the aisle seat if necessary. However, one person sat in the aisle seat, which I always thought was a dick move. Now, if someone wanted to sit next to this jack off, they would need to ask him to move so they could take a seat. People often act like the bus is more of their private limo than public transit and that entitlement really made me upset.

I found a set of empty seats in the next to last row, and nobody was in front of or behind me. Still, out of habit, I took out my headphones, put them in my ears, and gazed out the window. It looked like it could be summer. There was no snow on the ground and no frost on the windshields, but when we drove by someone you could see the anguish in their eyes. There was no way this could be happening this early in the year. It was a deep cold. Down to the bone. The kind of cold that hurts after just a few minutes. It wasn't below freezing yet, but it felt like it was.

After about two stops, a larger couple got on the bus and waddled to the back together. We all smiled cordially at each other, and they sat in the two empty seats in front of me. The headphones gave the couple a false sense of security, and they continued their personal conversation they were having before entering the bus in low, hushed tones.

"I just don't want to talk about this anymore," the man muttered under his breath. His tone did not match the happy face he was forcing. His voice was angry, like a father reprimanding a child, but his face was soft, warm, and understanding.

Her face, however, seemed to accurately match the conversation. She glared at him. A glare I recognized because Linda had given it to me countless times in the past. She clearly disagreed, and her face said that this conversation was not close to being over and that it didn't matter that they were in public, or on a bus, hell they could have been at the dinner table with his parents, because the look in her eyes told him they were finishing this conversation now.

"I just asked you a simple question," she hissed, her eyes piercing into him.

"And I already answered it. Three times. I don't want to talk about it." His face began to harden matching hers.

"Why can't you just answer the question?" She said looking around the bus to see if anyone had caught onto their argument yet.

"Because I shouldn't be on trial for anything!"

Some variation of this line was one I often used with Linda. It's a fair point. Even though I had no context, I'd still agree with the man. He wasn't on trial. And maybe I was projecting, but if he's anything like me, he's a loyal husband who doesn't cheat, doesn't do anything shady, leaves his phone unlocked, tries his best at his marriage, and he has this to deal with this kind of bullshit. A partner who just wants more and more and more. An engine that needs an oil change every week. A black hole of attention.

"I am allowed to ask questions," she snarled.

"Please don't make me fight on the goddamn bus, this is humiliating."

"I don't give a fuck."

I could see the frustration building, and I could tell he was becoming more and more tense.

"I'm begging you to stop this, ok?"

"I just want to know why you were texting my co-worker at 10:30 last night."

At this point, I realized I was doing a little too much projecting, and potentially, the man and myself had nothing actually in common. I got in trouble for a lot of stupid shit in my time with Linda. We had been together since we met at my party back when I was a junior in college. We had fought about anything and everything; money, spending too much time on my phone, coming home too late, coming home too early, not coming home at all, drinking too much, family, pets, exercise, we have even argued about arguing too much. I will say that regardless of our issues we had never been a couple to accuse the other of cheating. So, if someone was keeping score, Linda and I were better than the couple who accused each other of fooling around with each other's coworkers while on a city bus.

The man suddenly grabbed the yellow cord, and the bell rang letting the bus driver know to pull over to let someone off. From my count, they had been on for about two total stops.

"What are you doing?" The woman exclaimed, much louder than she had wanted to.

"I'd rather walk to work in this shit weather than spend another second getting embarrassed on a city bus!" He yelled. With that, he pushed the side doors open and got off, zipping up his jacket and walking into the fierce wind.

The woman started to silently cry in her seat. Everyone pretended like they didn't notice, but they did.

11

"Gawd, I just *love* living in Noo York," she slurred, downing a glass of red wine.

"That's great, Cindy," Linda said unenthused.

"You two have to come out and visit me!" She said emphatically. "There's just never a dull moment. There's always a new restaurant to try, or an art exhibit to see, new urban wineries, and museums. Who could forget it also has the best pizza in the world!"

I was losing interest in Cindy's non-stop 'Noo York' talk. She had moved out of Minneapolis eight months ago and had somehow already picked up the accent. Almost on cue, she looked at me and said, "I need to grab some wada." She went off into the kitchen and poured herself a glass of tap water.

I looked around the room, bored and hoping that soon Linda would want to go home. A, "Welcome Home Cindy," banner was strewn across the living room with some balloons and confetti peppered around. There was a cheap plastic backdrop of the New York City skyline against the wall, and apples were all over the apartment. They were hanging from the ceiling, they were in bowls, they were in the food, there were cutouts of apples on almost every wall in the house. Initially, I didn't get it, and when I asked Linda, she explained that it was because of, "The Big Apple." I felt dumb that I didn't make the connection, but I figured the decoration itself was also pretty stupid.

This was, what I would categorize as, an adult party. A little get together in Cindy's parents' house so she can try and throw in our faces how great her life is and how mundane ours had become. Look at Cindy! The world traveler! The talk of the town! How could one person surround herself with so many unique and interesting people?!

This party was a real who's who of people I don't give a shit about.

I wasn't fooled by any of this. Almost bi-weekly for the last few months, Cindy was calling Linda on the brink of tears. She explained how she missed home and her friends and would whimper about how miserable and small it was in her studio apartment in Brooklyn. How she wanted to eat at Annie's Parlor, her favorite burger place, and drink Surly beer. How terrible it was to ride the subway with groceries. The burdensome cost of eating out regularly. The impossibility of dating and meeting men in a big city. This party was all some big rouse. A charade. A trick of someone, too proud to admit they made a mistake and too embarrassed to simply move back, plays on everyone.

"Steven!" I heard a voice say in the doorway. I turned around to see a familiar face. White guy, glasses, brown hair, beard, brown eyes, same as everyone else. I put a smile on and quickly said, "Hey man!" and shook the guy's hand. "How have you been?" I asked.

"Pretty good," the white guy replied.

"Where are you working now?"

"What do you mean?" The white guy gave me a confused look. "I'm a teacher, I've been a teacher since we've met. I'm still at the same school."

"Shit, man," I said apologetically. "I'm sorry, I must have gotten you confused with someone else."

"What's my name?" The white guy asked sternly.

"Josh?" I said without hesitation.

"It's Zack."

"Same thing," I said half joking.

"Not even close to the same thing."

"It kind of is."

I laughed. Zack didn't.

"I'm just fucking with you, Zack."

"You're an asshole," Zack said as he made his way to the kitchen. He didn't yell it, but he said it loud enough for everyone in the room to hear it. Partygoers shot some glances, but I downed my drink and proceeded to make my way to the pony keg in the corner for another beer.

"Don't ruin this night for Cindy," I heard Linda say from behind me.

"That wasn't my intention."

"Why can't you just be nice to Zack? You know him and Cindy used to date before the move to New York."

"No. I really didn't."

"We went on a double date with them. You were there."

"That doesn't mean I remember the guy. Apparently, I met him once at a dinner a long time ago, and he was boring enough to forget. Cut me some slack."

I immediately turned around to fill my cup. I didn't have to see Linda to know what face she was making. I knew her well after a few years of marriage. As I topped off my beer, I heard her politely storm away as other guests civilly only partially stared.

I finished pouring my beer and stared at the, "Welcome Home Cindy," banner. It was a nice gesture by her parents to throw a party. My parents wouldn't do anything like this if I came home for a visit. Still, what was this? A five-year-old's birthday party?

I knew I shouldn't have been on such a high horse, and I wish that I could say I was better than Cindy. We were in the same boat. My marriage was on the rocks. We had each made a terrible mistake, and we were too ashamed to backtrack. Linda and I took vows. We exchanged rings. We said it in front of everyone. Cindy had declared herself independent. She was a new person. She couldn't come back. The pictures are on Facebook.

I noticed Cindy was sullenly sipping her glass of water away from everyone, and in that moment, I understood how Cindy actually felt. I didn't want to judge her anymore. I pitied her predicament. It's humiliating to post online to everyone you have met, both insignificant and meaningful, you're making a new life for yourself in a new city and less than a year later everybody knows you're giving up. My marriage was no different. Jackson had temporarily steadied the ship, but it was teetering again.

I went into the kitchen, grabbed a fresh glass, and picked up the only red wine that was open. It was a blend called Two Sailboats. The branding was unique, and generally, I don't see so much color on wine labels. There was a beautiful deep blue for the ocean, an orange-yellow sunset, and far off in the distance, you could see two masts sailing directly into the horizon where the sun was setting. I usually only saw names of vineyards in cursive or bold letters. I started pouring it, not the heavy pour I was used to, but a drink a respectable person would have with a sensible, family dinner.

Zack was in the kitchen and was passive aggressively telling anyone who would listen how much of a dick I was. He did it in the unique, Minnesota way, where he would talk just loud enough so you could hear your name, but just quiet enough that you wouldn't know what he was actually saying about you. I gave him a friendly wave, and he just glared back at me.

I went back into the living room and saw Cindy was still alone. I walked up to her and gave her the glass. She took it, surprised that I had noticed she was without a drink.

"You know," I started, "I'm proud of you for moving to New York."

She took a sip and smiled, "Really?" She asked.

"Of course. It takes a lot of guts to move to a new place and take a big step like that. Most people would never actually go through with it."

"Thanks, Steve," she said, brimming with some new confidence.

"Just know, that no matter what happens after, Linda and your family still care about you."

Cindy cocked her head to the side, "What do you mean?"

"Well, you know," I fumbled, "when you change your mind about where you want to live and-"

"What do you mean 'when'?" Cindy asked, getting frustrated.

"Forget I said anything," I replied, starting to walk away.

"No," she said sternly grabbing my sleeve, "that was a really fucked up thing to say."

"Ok, Cindy. I'm sorry. Please, let go of my arm. I genuinely didn't mean to offend you. I was just saying that no matter what you decide to do we support you."

"Why? Do you think I am going to come back here?"

"I never said that."

"You know what, Steve? Linda is right about you." Her volume had continued to crescendo into a yell. "You're an asshole. You just walk around like everybody owes you something. Like you're better than everyone else. And why? Because you married Linda? Because you hate your office job she helped you get? Because you're some brooding intellectual who just can't make his personality fit in with the rest of us?"

Linda had come inside the backdoor with a group of friends to most likely sneak a cigarette. I saw her laughing and joking until she made eye contact with me and she exhaled deeply. She immediately started making her way to where Cindy was berating me.

"You know what the worst part is? Linda used to be a strong and independent person, and you fucked it all up. You ruined her. I don't know how, but you have killed my best friend because of your stupid bullshit."

"What's going on?" Linda asked hushed and tense, trying to get whatever was happening resolved quickly.

"Nothing," I replied, "I was just going to get you so we could leave."

Cindy, in one swift motion, brought her wine glass back, then thrust it forward. I didn't try and move. I just watched as her red wine left the glass and went directly onto my chest at the top of my light blue shirt. People were politely watching out of the corners of their eyes because of the argument that was ensuing, but now that Cindy had purposefully spilled wine all over me, all Minnesota pleasantries were out the window. People were staring directly at us. Some of them holding back laughter, some scared, some angry.

I looked at Linda. She wasn't making eye contact with either of us anymore. Her head was hung low, her face mostly hidden, but I could see tears coming down the side of her cheeks, and she was sniffling quietly. After a few moments Linda lifted her head and wiped the tears from her face, and her expression was one I had never seen before. Still, it was identifiable. At first, I thought it was just sadness or some embarrassment, but she was ashamed. I know some people use those two words interchangeably, but until you see someone truly ashamed of you, it becomes clear there's a big difference.

Linda surveyed the room and saw everyone standing around and looking directly at us. She looked at them all for just a brief second and without hesitating any longer, and without saying another word, she briskly walked out the front door and slammed it behind her. The sound echoed in the room, and everyone stood frozen. First not breaking eye contact with the door, and then slowly moving their gaze towards me.

My eyes began to sting, and I wiped my face in an attempt to squeegee some of the liquid off. I shook my hand letting a few red droplets stain the white carpet.

"Please, don't do that," Cindy said, annoyed she even had to bring it up.

I didn't reply. I again got the wine off me and shook the remnants onto the floor, further staining the carpet all while I looked at Cindy. I then calmly walked to the door leaving a trail of red splotches along the way. When I put my hand on the doorknob, I wanted to turn around and make some sort of smart-ass comment. I was so close to saying, "Welcome home, Cindy," or, "Great seeing you again," but I didn't. I just went out into the cool night and meandered toward the car shaking wine off the whole way.

It had been on my bucket list to get a drink thrown on my face at some point in my life. I just didn't think it would be in front of a bunch of people I knew at an adult party. I always figured it would have occurred more in a dive bar setting.

12

We got home, and I slowly closed and locked the door behind us. There wasn't any sound in the apartment aside from Jackson scurrying to the front door, looking for his dinner, which was now a few hours late. I knelt down and pet him, and he closed his eyes and buried his head in my palm. After a few pets, he let out a soft meow and scampered away through the kitchen and into the study. Linda walked into the living room, put her bag down on the couch and sighed. The tension was thick, and I could tell something was coming.

I went through the kitchen and down the hall to the bathroom and used an old towel to dry off my face. Then I splashed some warm water around my neck and wet my hair until I stopped seeing red wine circle the drain. I took off my shirt and threw it into the trash. It was too far gone. You have to get club soda on it immediately if you want a small blotch to come out, let alone an entire glass. I washed some of the sticky red wine off my chest until I was comfortably sure I had removed all of it. Satisfied, I went into the bedroom and changed into some basketball shorts and an old college t-shirt.

I went into the kitchen and took a mason jar out of the cabinet and gave myself a tall pour of red wine. I know it seems like I shouldn't want red wine after the evening I just had, but smelling it the whole way home really got me in the mood for it.

"Steve," Linda said softly, to nobody in the dark living room. The only visible part of her was the outline from the street lamps outside. I grabbed my glass and flicked on the lights; her silhouette turned to the discernable wife I knew. Her green eyes were watery and cold, and her body language was slumped and full of defeat and frustration. I could see the beginning of her crow's feet wrinkles next to her eyes because she had washed some of the foundation away with her tears. It was one of the few times I had seen her without a full face of makeup in years. She didn't look old without it, but I could see she was more weathered than I expected because of the stress of everyday life and of course me. I looked down at my hand and realized it was covered in kitten fur.

"I don't think I can do this anymore." It was such a strong sentence with such little thought or emotion behind it.

"Why?" I didn't want to argue. I asked just because I was interested what it was.

"I could see it in your face tonight. I know you were trying your best. I just need someone who cares about the people in my life. You just don't, and that's okay." The sentences seemed so robotic, like she was on autopilot. Just going through the motions of being alive.

"Are you sure?" I asked quietly.

Her eyes met mine and she slowly nodded. A singular tear fell down her cheek. She was a little sad, but she was a good enough person to at least not yell at me again. Decent enough to not make this whole experience a nightmare. She had the class to hide the excitement of a new life.

"I don't want you to just make this decision because of the arguments from tonight. I mean they were embarrassing, but I don't think that's why we should end a marriage."

"It's not just that." She briefly paused and wiped the tear from her cheek, "We just haven't been on the same page lately with anything. You aren't happy being around me or my friends or family, and I don't like the way your life is heading."

I could have picked a fight here, but what's the point?

"Besides," she started again, "don't you think it would be better for the two of us? You wouldn't have to go to therapy or see any of my friends again."

"Why are you trying to sell this to me? You're the one asking for a separation."

She shrugged her shoulders. After a few minutes that dragged on, I asked the question we were both thinking, "What now?"

She had the same reaction. She just shrugged her shoulders and stared at me blankly. I sat down on the couch and Jackson ran to me, jumped up, and curled into my lap.

"I'm going to pack some of my stuff and stay with my parents," she said after a few moments. She put her hand on my shoulder and walked out of the living room. Jackson rolled onto his back, showing his belly and still purring softly.

Hardly Harding

WINTER

1

"I'm going to have to write you up again," Jim said sternly.

"That's fine. I'm late, so I get it," I replied.

"You're not just late Steven. You're nearly three hours late. If you don't watch it, you'll be on probation."

"Ok."

"And once you're on probation we'll have to start the process of-"

I had already started walking away.

I went into my office and closed the door. The last few months had left me disheveled and lost. Not directly because of Linda, but because of all the issues that stem from starting a divorce. The lawyers, documents, statements, financial holdings, money, friends, public humiliation, it was all wearing me down. It didn't help that I was burning my bridges, as I was becoming the cautionary tale of what not to do while going through a separation, or break-up, or whatever you want to call it. I was showing up to work late, I wasn't exercising or shaving, I was blowing off friends and family, and I was drinking heavily and regularly.

Per state law, they require a cooling-off period of six long months before the divorce could be finalized. I had no hope or intention of rekindling the marriage, which made it increasingly more difficult for me to get away with work infractions. Initially, Linda's father, Greg, thought we would be able to work through it. He came into my office the week after she got her stuff and moved in with her folks. He sat down in one of my leather chairs and looked down at the floor. I remember he said with distant, and unconcerned eyes, "I know you're going through a rough patch with Linda, and I don't want you to worry. This kind of thing happens from time to time. Marriage can be difficult, and you aren't the first guy to have to sleep on the couch for a while."

"Thanks," was all I replied.

He got up and left the room. That was one of the longest talks we ever had, and I hadn't seen or heard from him since then. He was probably more anxious though. The disciplinary actions against me were actually getting reported to HR. I was becoming a liability, and he knew it. Soon he wouldn't have a reason to protect me.

The sofa across from my desk still had the pillow I used to sleep on when Linda had kicked me out so she could get more of her belongings and I had to stay in the office for a few days. My eyes moved to the garbage can that still had some hair in it from when I shaved into it weeks earlier because the CEO was in town and I was too hungover that morning to do it at home. This whole office was a myriad of disappointment and depression. A tapestry of corporate nightmares. A shrine of what I never wanted to become. I looked at my watch. It was about 11:00 and I could tell I was done. I had only been there for ten or fifteen minutes, but I had enough. I opened my door and started to walk briskly toward the elevator.

"Where are you going?" I heard from behind me. It was the unmistakable, disappointed voice of Jim.

"I'm going to meet with a client," I replied without turning around.

"No, you're not!" He said, voice cracking. "What's his name? You'll be written up for this, Harding." I could tell he was serious because he used my last name.

The elevator opened, and I stepped inside. I turned around and saw Jim, red in the face, looking like he was about to burst from the seams. I pressed the button for the main floor and smiled at Jim.

"Don't you smile at me! You're just a privileged boy who married rich and is throwing a hissy fit about everything." I felt sorry for the guy. I mean, he was a real prick to work for, but he was just upset because I got away with this kind of behavior. He had gone to school, worked hard for good grades, sold insurance as an entry-level job just to be able to move up in this office. After years, and years, and years of hard work, showing up on time, and ass kissing he was finally given the smallest bit of reward. Just a pay raise and some employees underneath him. All I did was drop out of college and marry some executive's daughter, and I was only one rung below him. Even though that was our relationship on paper, he could never fire me. I was still untouchable. At least right now I was.

The door started to close, and I stopped it. I looked at the guy. I had seen him a million times, but he was always the same. Bald, beet red, obese. I always dismissed him because even though he was insufferable, he wasn't threatening. He was a bad boss, mostly for choosing battles like this one.

"You can start to process the paperwork," I said calmly. "I know it's another infraction, but I promise you won't have to deal with me much longer."

His gaze softened, and I could tell he was moving back to a more appropriate level of office temperament.

"You're not a bad guy," he said sympathetically, realizing he had crossed the line. "You just have to get your shit together fast."

"I know."

The automatic doors shut between us and the soft, descending hum washed over me.

2

My front door closed behind me, and Jackson had run out from a box he liked to sleep in near the radiator. Linda had taken almost everything from the apartment. Her parents had paid for most of it, so I didn't mind. She only left behind a twenty-five year-old recliner from her grandparent's cabin along with a card table that I was using as the dining room table. The only piece that I really disagreed with her taking was a bed that she had bought for Jackson. The day she left she said she was planning on taking him with her, which was also something I was okay with. However, when she tried to get him out of the apartment, he freaked out, and clawed at her. Then he ran away and hid. She had attempted multiple times to relocate him, but they had also not gone well. Jackson had no interest in leaving what was now his apartment. Eventually, Linda surrendered and left the cat here until we could figure out a way to get him to go with her.

There is something off about being a single guy with a cat. People look at you funny when you say it. Nobody cares if you have a dog, but a cat is almost unforgivable if you're a guy. I always thought it was weird because lots of successful men who had trouble with women loved cats. Bukowski, Hemingway, Kerouac, all loved cats and they were geniuses in their own rights. I mean, I haven't read their books, but it was a good comeback when people made fun of me.

Jackson rubbed against my legs and flicked his tail, happy to see me; Happy it wasn't Linda coming to try and take him away. Some animals are like that. They don't like being taken away from what they know. Or, they just don't appreciate someone trying to change everything. One of the two.

I turned to lock the door and saw the white corkboard Linda had been using to make sure I would remember wedding dates and other events I often forgot about. It had been picked clean except for a few receipts from Target and some old grocery list. There was a new yellow note pinned directly in the center of the board. Linda and I haven't spoken face-to-face since she moved out, and the most interaction we had were text messages, which were for emergency purposes only. I took the note down, and all it said was:

Be out Thursday 3-7

By far the most frustrating part of these notes was that Linda wasn't working and could easily come while I was supposed to be at the office. A small nuisance among dozens more in an attempt to break me. For what exactly, I really couldn't tell. I had run through all the scenarios. Perhaps this was an attempt to show power and demonstrate her ability to control my life after we were already separated. Maybe it was a way to nudge her way back into my life in an attempt to get us back together. Or maybe, and more realistically, she was just being a difficult pain in the ass just for the sake of it.

The important thing when going through a divorce isn't who is right or wrong. Nobody cares about that because, in America, the only thing we are interested in is the first person to act out. You can say whatever you want, but once someone lashes back, the person who blows up is automatically the one out of line. It's all just about retaliation. We don't have time for the full story.

Hockey has it right. You get time in the box for instigating, just like you get for fighting.

3

"You really should quit if this is how you are going to behave," John said before he even put down his laptop bag in our booth. Since Linda left, John and I met up every Tuesday. Before, we would merely meet whenever just to have a pleasant happy hour together. We used it as a way to unwind and talk shit about our jobs. Since John had actually gone through a divorce years before he preferred we meet up weekly. He had a rough time with his separation, and figured I was having trouble too. The underlying issue was I didn't feel that sadness he was always talking about. I wasn't happy, but I felt like myself.

John said this was undiagnosed depression, and I hadn't dealt with the issues yet. I needed to embrace the emotions, and he theorized that I was still going through the shock of losing my wife. It was going to hit me hard and soon, it would feel like my whole world was falling apart. He said for him, it was like when his childhood dog had died. Suddenly he was aware of mortality, and the ground had fallen out from underneath him. I know he thought he was doing me a favor, but these weekly meetings seemed to do him more good than me.

"Why do you think I need to quit?" I asked innocently.

"Let me stress, I don't think you should quit. I think you should get your shit together and start showing up to work on time. Because if you don't start doing your job, they're going to fire you. I heard Jim talking about it loudly in the lunchroom." John finally hung his jacket on the booth coat hanger and took a seat. I could tell he was serious. I could already read the writing on the wall.

"They can't fire me. And even if they wanted to, I don't think Linda's dad would let that fly until the divorce was finalized." I said this half sarcastically and half serious.

"Shouldn't you get out now then? Before the hammer comes down? A resignation always looks better than a termination."

"I'll just leave this one off my resume."

"You've been at this company for years. It's even worse having it blank than having a job you got fired from on there. A gap that large in work history looks really bad."

"John, at this point, I just don't care. This job is killing me. I have been looking for something new since before Linda left, and I don't see a lot of reason to actually stick around. I'm not getting anything I want out of this company. This isn't a stepping stone or training for the next path I want to take. It's just an endless, winding trail to nowhere. Does that make sense?"

This statement made John visibly upset, which is something I rarely saw in him. He was an odd character, but he was gregarious and silly.

"Steve, you know some of us actually have to work at that company. Not all of us get the luxury of marrying into an executive's family, and we can't show up whenever we want or do as little work as we feel like. I have seen you come in hungover and late more times than I can even count with almost no consequences. How in the hell could this job be killing you?"

All of these were fair points. I totally understood where he was coming from. He was someone who worked hard and deserved the right to criticize me for my laziness and ineptitude at managing people or selling insurance. He still believed Linda was the root of my issues.

"I can't really explain it," I replied. "This whole thing feels like some sort of rouse, but it's not. I feel like everything I have done, that I have achieved, is just completely void of any meaning or significance."

After a long break, John broke the silence. "People would kill to have what has been given to you. You have a good job, a wife you could probably get back if you would call her, a nice apartment, friends. Don't get me wrong, this isn't a perfect situation, but it is a situation that is better than ninety-five percent of the people I know."

I couldn't tell if that statement was an attempt at complimenting me or was more of John doing some self-loathing.

"I appreciate the advice and guidance John, I really do. I understand that you have gone through it before, and you have a good perspective about all of this. But that is all what happened to *you*. My marriage and divorce aren't like yours. My future isn't like yours. Most importantly, I feel like I need to say that this is my decision. That is somehow getting lost with everyone telling me what my next steps have to be."

"We're just trying to help you," John interjected.

"I don't want any more help."

John shook his head, disappointed in everything I was saying. He looked at me, desperation in his eyes, frustration on his face, almost begging me to listen.

"Sorry, John," I said.

He got up, put his coat on, and grabbed his laptop bag.

"Are you leaving? We just got here."

"If you aren't going to listen to what I have to say, there's no point in us doing this every week," he snapped.

"So, unless I agree with you and do what you say, you won't get a beer with me? Isn't this supposed to be for me?"

John didn't react. He just adjusted the laptop bag across his chest and took his beanie out of his jacket pocket, pushing it down hastily on his head, and walked out the front door. Cold air rushed into the bar, and everyone grimaced. The waitress came by and put my beer on the table.

"Still want this?" She asked.

I didn't reply. I just started to drink it.

4

I stepped out of Dan Kelly's Pub after just a few. Drinking by yourself at home is, for some reason, less socially acceptable than drinking at a bar alone. One Easter a few years ago, Linda and I got into a rough argument that resulted in me going to a local dive bar. The place was nearly empty except for a few regulars that I doubt ever missed a day going there. Easter is an odd holiday to get drunk publicly on. Christmas, New Years, Thanksgiving, Fourth of July, your birthday, all of those are fine, but Easter?

Regardless, I sat in a booth in the back, I ordered their blue plate special which was a slice of ham, some macaroni and cheese, and mashed potatoes for five dollars, and sat alone for four or so hours, drinking and listening to podcasts. Multiple people came up to my table and asked if I wanted to join them, but I declined. By the time I left the bar and turned my phone off airplane mode, I had dozens of text messages from Linda and my Mom wondering where I was and if I was ok. That was a pivotal moment in our relationship. I could have saved all this time and energy I was going through if I had just mustered the courage to actually walk away from her that night.

The sun was already setting, and the air felt cold and heavy with no wind to stir it up. I passed a small group of friends who were all laughing and smoking near the entrance in an alley as I headed toward home. I could take the bus, but I figured a nice, brisk walk through downtown would be enjoyable. There wasn't a rush to get home, and I thought the fresh air would do me some good.

I'm not sure why, but I thought back to a night Linda and I had experienced as newlyweds. A night that had been riddled with red flags, but I had brushed them all off as things that happen sometimes. I should have been able to tell that the interactions I was having showed I didn't belong with the crowd I had married into.

5

"This spread isn't bad," the man next to me said.

"Yeah, it's fine," I replied.

He scoffed, taking me for a snob, which was a fair assessment. This party was a stage for something. Linda had explained on the way here that it was for someone's birthday, or wedding, or going away party. I couldn't keep them all straight. All I knew was that I was here, with a morbidly obese man at the food table, looking at a layout of the most whitewashed, dull food. It was all sandwich triangles, shrimp cocktails, and stuffed mushrooms. It was a table for someone who wanted to look wealthy but didn't have the money for it.

The house itself was nice, but that's only because $400,000 can buy a big, new home thirty minutes outside of most cities. I'm sure they poured even more money they didn't have into doing unnecessary remodeling, and the husband just agreed to make his wife stop nagging him about it. I bet he tried to do it on his own for a while, and I bet he failed. Miserably.

Linda would drag me to these regularly. People would admire the house, comment on the food, kiss cheeks, and say how long it's been, but this kind of party was just a way for the host to show off her new place. Bring your own beer, drive way out the middle of nowhere, but the food is free.

The obese man at the table piled his plate with shrimp and sandwiches, skipping the fruit and veggie platters and sauntered away, happy with his haul. I continued to look at the food for a few moments. I considered my options and took a small plate of celery and carrots. I usually am not the kind of person who watches what I eat, but after seeing a man nearly have a heart attack looking at food, it significantly diminished my appetite.

"Steven." I heard Linda say softly behind me.

I turned around, and she was standing there, wine in hand, looking at my plate of food. She gave me a puzzled look because of my selection, but I just shrugged my shoulders.

"Would you be able to drive home?" She asked suddenly.

"If I need to."

"Are you going to have fun if you can't drink?"

"Yes."

"Ok, I'm just making sure."

"Worst comes to worst, we'll just Uber home."

She glared at me.

"Fine. I will make sure I can drive home."

She got close and kissed me. Then, she went off into a group of women and said something that made them all laugh loudly in unison. If I was going to have a drink, I needed to get out of the house and try and find some sort of secluded, quiet place where Linda wouldn't be judgmentally watching me, and I could steer clear of any more conversations.

I had to make a move fast, while she was distracted. I noticed there was a door that led to a newly built deck outside that had a big, blue cooler. I figured it was the best shot I had of drinking a beer in peace, so I quickly slinked outside into the chilly evening.

Once outside, I popped the cooler open and found an array of cheap domestic beers. It wasn't my first choice, but I could make it work. I pulled one out randomly from the middle that felt nice and cold and opened it as I surveyed the backyard. The relaxing ambiance music from the party inside mixed with muffled laughter and conversation seemed like background noise from a movie.

As I made my way down the stairs into the grass, through the dim light, I could see cheap, newly planted, flowers that lined the fence. I strolled for about fifteen yards when I heard the door open, and shut quietly behind me, the party noise getting louder and quieter as the stranger came outside. I only say, "stranger," because I didn't want to turn around and see Linda standing there, arms crossed, ready to yell at me about having a light beer at a party.

Then I heard the cooler open, ice being mixed around, and a sharp cracking open of a new beer. I realized this wasn't Linda. She would come out to see what I was doing in the yard, but she wouldn't have picked any of those anonymous light beers.

I heard steps start to get louder behind me, and I turned around to see a well-built thirty-something year-old man with a beer in his hand coming toward me. He had a receding hairline and thick glasses, but he seemed well kept and smiled wide.

"Admiring the yard?" He said, beaming with pride.

"Yeah, it's a good setup."

"I hope you don't mind me coming out here. My wife set this party up and truthfully, I am not a big fan of things like this. I figured I would be the only one out here."

We both awkwardly took a sip of our beer, not knowing what to say to one another. Also, I couldn't tell what exactly was the truth with him. On the one hand, if Linda and I were to throw a party like this, displaying success and a new home, I know I would have to do it regardless of what I wanted.

On the other hand, this is the general line people say when they are trying to humbly brag. You can't say you wanted to have a party to show off because that makes you look like an asshole. That's why we call them housewarming parties, and movie premiers, and graduations because those are the most polite way to shove accomplishments in someone else's face.

"What's your name again?" He asked.

"Steve. Yours?"

"Ian," he said, extending his arm for a handshake. I shook it half-heartedly and stared back at the plants lining his fence. I glanced back at him after a few seconds and politely said, "You look kind of familiar. Did you go to Central High School?"

"No, I'm not from the Cities," he said, his smile growing larger. "But you probably recognize me because I am kind of famous."

I laughed. Not because he wasn't famous, and not because I thought this might be a joke. I laughed because it was such an odd statement. I could immediately tell he didn't appreciate my reaction, as his wide grin turned into a tightly lipped scowl. He wasn't mad, but I could see the response had bruised his ego quite a bit.

"What are you famous for?" I asked, genuinely curious.

"Well," he started, a little embarrassed, "my family has owned and operated Maden's Hardware up near Saint Cloud for the last two generations."

"I'm sorry," I said, not sure why I was apologizing, "I don't spend much time up near Saint Cloud."

"Well, Maden's has branched out now. We're just outside Minneapolis, and we want to get within the city within the next few years."

"I'm sorry Ian, I still don't understand what any of this has to do with you being famous."

"With that attempt to branch out, comes a lot of advertising money. So, the family has poured tens of thousands of dollars into TV and billboards." That smile started to come back across Ian's face as he said this.

"Oh, so you're on the billboards and commercials then."

"See, I told you I was kind of famous," he exclaimed exuberantly, and figuring I had finally remembered him.

"I'm sorry Ian, I have never heard of your family's hardware store, and I have never seen a commercial or a billboard for it."

"Have you been living under a rock? They're everywhere."

"Sorry," I replied, still apologizing for no reason while I shifted my weight uncomfortably.

"Well, what do you do?" He asked in a taunting tone.

"I work in insurance."

"Oh! Wow! Big insurance man has never heard of a family owned business from outside the big city. Hicks like me better be careful around big shots like you."

"I didn't mean to insult you, Ian. I just haven't seen the advertisements is all." I calmly reassured him.

"Well then, you must not do a lot of work on your house, Steve, because we're one of the biggest family-owned hardware stores in the state."

I started to laugh again at the insanity of this interaction.

"Oh, you think this is funny now? You know what Steve, I do know you're married to Linda, and without her, you'd be some nobody. You wouldn't be invited to housewarming parties, or going away parties for people traveling abroad. You'd just be some loser working some dead-end job."

"That's weird, I feel like I could say the same thing for you if your family hadn't opened a hardware store."

Even through the dim lighting from his porch, I could tell from his expression I wouldn't be welcome at this party much longer. Ian turned around, marched inside, and slammed the sliding glass door. Now that he was in his home, I could see the anger seething from him. The dark red color, the clenched fists, the caveman hunch of a person enraged. He didn't turn away either, and for a while he just sat in his doorway, staring at me through the glass. Which made it even weirder because through the darkness of the backyard there was no way he could see very much of me or my body language.

I was the first to turn away, and I walked further away from the house, appreciating the landscaping and silence, still feeling the seething rage of a scorned, new homeowner behind me. I tried to ignore it and, after a few minutes I glanced back, and he was gone. I sighed, relieved that he wasn't going to come back and take out some sort of revenge on me.

I knew how this would play out. Ian would find his wife. She would immediately ask him what's wrong, and he would tell her his side of the story; that he was a welcoming and helpful host, and his hospitality was met immediately with hostility and rudeness. In this situation, who are they going to side with? The guy giving them free food and booze, or the guy insulting the homeowner? It was an open and shut case. I would be found guilty by a jury of my peers.

Just then, I heard the porch door quietly slide open, just a little, and quickly shut. I turned around and saw the frame of a slender, blonde woman come out of the house. I knew who it was. For some reason, at that moment, it brought me back to that first night we met. In that shitty house, with the friends I don't talk to anymore, when the only thing that mattered was her and me, in the dark with cigarettes and Styx.

I started walking toward her, and I could already tell it was going to be rough. I didn't even have to see her face, I could tell from the speed at which she was coming toward me. When Linda was within a few feet of me, I saw heads peeping out of windows and through the sliding glass door, and I heard a squish. I looked down and saw that she had stepped in the most enormous pile of dog shit I had seen in my entire life.

6

I came home to a hungry meow and a dash of paws across the wood floor to greet me. Jackson had started to lose a lot of his independence, and it was becoming clear from the rapidly diminishing visits, in both length and volume, from Linda that he was growing less dependent on her. I picked him up, and he purred lightly as I cradled him like a baby. My nose was numb, and my face felt chapped from the cold, dry air outside.

"I thought you were allergic." I heard a voice blandly say from the kitchen. It didn't scare me, it was just unexpected and cut the silence of the apartment so sharply that I almost dropped Jackson, startled initially that it might be a burglar. After a second I realized, how many burglars are aware of your allergies?

"You know what, I think I have grown a bit more immune to my cat allergy," I said peering around the corner to see Linda, sitting in the dining room. She half turned to see me holding a cat I had initially and vehemently protested.

"You look great!" She said smiling sincerely.

"Thanks," I replied, "I honestly just cut back on the beer." I lied.

There was a look of disappointment in her eyes. She had always nagged me to not drink so much but never was able to get me to do it. I had done it on my own. In a way, I know she secretly wanted me to be drinking more since we were going through a rough patch. But she was too good of a person to ever admit it. This feeling was abruptly cut short by her realizing the apartment was riddled with old bottles and cans. Still, she got up from the old card table and walked up to me.

"Steve," she started coyly, "I don't know if this whole separation thing is a good idea." She reached for Jackson to pet him on the head, but he ducked low to avoid it. He pushed himself off my chest and clunked ungraciously to the ground and scampered across the floor into his room. "Father says you have been struggling at work and you aren't even trying to do your job. Jim has apparently written a stack of reports against you, and soon, Dad won't be able to protect you anymore."

A silence hung in the air for what seemed like a long time. It matched the dark, dreary apartment lit only by the overhanging kitchen light Linda was standing under.

"Why?" I asked.

"Why what?"

"Why would we do this again? Why would you show up now? Why would you gut the apartment and then come back and say now you wanted to figure everything out months later? What would be the point?"

"Because I'm worried about you, Steve," she said convincingly.

"Why?"

This line of questioning wasn't one she was expecting. What she expected was to come to the apartment, make this statement, and then I would take her back with absolutely no questions asked. Why wouldn't I? What did I have to lose? Look at what I had to gain.

"Steve, I just want to go back to before I left. I want to be married, and I want to live here with you and Jackson. Now isn't good for you and me to be apart." She motioned to the empty, beer can riddled space around her, "Look at what is happening. The drinking. The messy apartment. The job that is nearly impossible to be fired from, yet you're somehow managing to do it. You're in such a rut you can't even get to work on time, and you're leaving early every day. Whether you want to admit it or not, you are depressed, and I don't think you're dealing with this situation like an adult."

"Don't take this the wrong way Linda, but you don't know in the least bit what is wrong with me or how my career is going. And for someone who doesn't have a job, I find this very unfair."

"I know father will fire you if you don't take me back," she replied in a snotty tone.

"Good."

Linda looked surprised. She thought this enormous effort would be enough for me to want to go back to our old life and was confident that when she walked into the apartment, she could effortlessly slip back into how we used to be. After all, Linda thought she had the upper hand, but after just five minutes of conversation, she was already trying to play dirty.

"Linda, you can think and say whatever you want about me to make yourself feel better. You can call me lazy, messy, unable to keep a job, whatever helps you sleep better at night is ok with me."

There was a blank expression on her face that was as empty as the apartment. Linda always got her way until tonight. She grabbed her purse off the kitchen counter and started to walk out of the light, and she was almost invisible when she turned around and said, "You know, I feel bad for you because you have no idea what you're turning away."

I was about to respond when I realized this was my chance to take the high road. I smiled, nodded my head and quietly muttered, "Good night, Linda."

She stomped out of the apartment and slammed the front door behind her. I walked into the barely visible living room and locked the door behind her as I heard the car peeling out of the parking lot. It was then I saw Jackson's face peer out of his room. He ran to me and rubbed on my legs, purring loudly in the empty apartment. I pet him gently on his head, and he closed his eyes, rolling onto his back and exposing his small belly. After a few moments, I went to his food bowl and filled it up to the brim, and he sprinted over to it, devouring as much and as fast as he could.

"I promise, Jackson," I said as he inhaled his food, "no matter how bad this situation gets, you'll get your kibbles."

Jackson looked at me, like he was half understanding, mouth full of food and some dropping back into his bowl.

7

The bus was half empty, but I made an elderly man, sitting in the aisle seat, get up so I could take the window seat. This visibly annoyed him, but what was more inconsiderate than making him move was his attitude that he had the right to box out another bus rider, just because he sat where he did.

"It's so warm for a winter morning," the old man said, trying to entice me into a conversation.

"It sure is," I said smiling, putting my earbuds in.

He gave a disappointed look and started to utter something else, but the earbuds blocked out the sound even though nothing was playing. Still, the old man's observation was correct. Warm in Minnesota in early November is still cold relative to everywhere else. So cold in fact that we were getting the snow which the city has become incredibly good at ignoring. I watched the snow fall gracefully outside the bus window. The sun wasn't entirely up yet, and it was still dark in the early hours of the morning.

The bus was quiet, and I started to doze off as it rocked me into a light sleep. Clearly, I couldn't continue to work as a manager at this or any company. Not only did it make me miserable to be in an office setting, but I was unfit to lead anyone at this juncture in my life.

As I watched the snow build into small mounds on the side of the road, my phone vibrated in my pocket. It was a text from my Mom. "We missed you last night at dinner. Everything ok?"

I hadn't been to the family dinner since Linda had left several months ago. It was going to be a whole thing with them. I could already see their inauthentic, faces filled with imitated sympathy as they said half-heartedly told me that everything happens for a reason. That the Harding family would stick together and prevail through anything as long as we didn't separate. There are so many other fish in the sea. Some other cliché. Etcetera, etcetera, etcetera.

I put the phone back in my pocket and ignored it. Even though the Harding family could get through anything, none of them had come to visit me. I don't mean since the divorce train started picking up steam but ever. People only want relationships that are easy for them, when in reality it would be best if we sometimes tried to push ourselves in uncomfortable but better situations.

The bus came to a squeaky stop, and another elderly man came onboard. The old man sitting next to me was significantly different than this one though, in more ways than one. The gentleman sitting adjacent to me looked purposeful. The kind of guy who doesn't need to work, but does it anyways for fulfillment, or to get out of the house, or to just not lose purpose. He was dressed in a tweed jacket and had thick rimmed, circular glasses on. His eyes were magnified and sharp.

The guy who boarded the bus seemed bewildered and aloof. After a few seconds of confusion about the price of the ride, which hadn't changed in several years, the driver just motioned him to go take a seat in frustration. He surveyed the available seats for a moment and shuffled his way to the back across the aisle from where the old man and I were sitting. He gingerly sat down and smiled at the man sitting next to me.

"Hello, Frank!" The newer old man said.

"Victor," the man next to me replied, nodding without making eye contact.

"I haven't seen you around lately," Victor said.

"I've been busy," Frank replied quietly. His demeanor had changed drastically since trying to talk to me when I got onto the bus. Originally, his body language was relaxed and open. He was trying to start up a conversation and was smiling before I had shut him out. Now, his demeanor had closed off, and he wasn't making eye contact with anyone.

"What have you been up to?" Victor asked.

"Nothing," Frank replied without looking over.

"That's not what I heard." Victor responded.

"Well, you shouldn't believe everything you hear," snapped Frank.

"I'm just saying, Frank. We're here to help you if you need it. That's all."

Frank turned and looked at the man sitting across the aisle from us. I couldn't see his facial expression when he was looking at Victor, but if it was anything like what it was when he turned and faced the front of the bus once again, it was one of cold indifference. Frank reached across me and pulled the yellow cord to stop the bus. He grabbed his things and made his way to the front.

"You still got my number?" Victor asked.

Frank nodded without looking back and walked off into the cold morning air.

A look of disappointment and frustration came across his face as he watched Frank aimlessly wander into the Minneapolis side streets.

"You just can't help some people," Victor said under his breath.

8

"Steve, I need to see you in my office," Jim said sternly. He didn't look how he usually did when he had to take me somewhere for a private talk. Sure, there was that hard ass face, with his no-nonsense mustache, but there was a glint of joy in his eyes.

"Good, I wanted to talk to you too, Jim," I replied. This visibly surprised him. He knew I would avoid conversation with him at every possible opportunity. I didn't mean to, but I threw him off his game. We walked me to his office, and he closed the door behind us. I sat down across from him as he shuffled through a stack of disorganized papers that were strewn along his desk.

"You are late again, Steven," he said authoritatively as he pulled one of the papers off his desk. 'This is your third write up in two weeks, and I have let this fly countless times in the last few months as well."

"Yeah, today was kind of a weird morning for me though. Some old guys-"

"I don't give a shit, Harding!" He exclaimed, "Every day it's a new excuse. Every day it's a new reason as to why I should care about you being special. Just because you married into the right family doesn't mean they'll protect you forever."

His eyes looked sharp, and he was almost foaming at the mouth. You know when somebody is really passionate about something? The intensity people get when they are really into a conspiracy theory or when somebody has been brainwashed by the culture of a new business they started working for. It's a kind of tunnel vision that blocks out other perspectives and points of view that just make the person seem crazy. You're trying your best, sitting there listening to them talk about the petrodollar or chemtrails, but none of it is sinking in, because you don't have a stake in it; and you don't have a stake in it because you don't buy it.

"I'm just going to stop you there, Jim." I could tell he was going to completely lose it. If I rode it out and let him berate me for another ten minutes, I would be able to sue this company for some sort of professional misconduct. That would be the smart move. I would be able to settle out of court, take a significant lump sum, and move to Mexico. Sometimes though, regardless of a potential profit margin, it is best to speak your mind. Besides, just sitting there seemed like way too much work.

"This place just isn't conducive to my long-term goals. I'm going to go ahead and quit." Jim froze. I have said some ludicrous things to him in the past, but he didn't expect this.

"E-excuse me?" He stammered.

"I want to quit. This place isn't helping me get to where I need to be."

"And where is that exactly?" Jim said mockingly.

"I don't know."

"You do realize, that because you are quitting and not getting fired we won't be paying you severance." He laughed intermittently as this came out of his mouth.

"I don't care."

I stood up and opened the door behind me and started walking out of the office. As I took my third step into the hallway, I heard him fumbling for the phone to ask for security to escort me out, but by the time they would be there. I would be at the bus stop, thinking about what to do with all this free time.

Of course, I would be lying if I said that I did all of this because of my ex-wife, or to get back at my father-in-law, or whatever else people say the underlying reason is. It also isn't true that I did it all because I hated the job because after all, it was a very easy, well-paying position where I could do whatever I wanted. Ultimately, maybe I could tell I was getting fired, and I am just not big enough of a person to allow Jim that last piece of joy. Realistically, I think it is fair to say I left because of all of those reasons.

After just a few minutes, I was at the corner as a bus squealed to a halt and I got on. It wasn't mine, but I didn't have anywhere to be.

9

"Is this the part of the story where you give me your watch and tell me I have always been your best friend and you warn me not to go to work tomorrow?" John seemed overly pleased and prepared to bust my balls. I bet he practiced it at work in the handicap bathroom mirror so he could get that delivery just right. John took a big swig of his beer, and I could see the smile through the bottom of his glass.

"No, John. It's not like that at all. Mostly I just came because this is our weekly ritual."

"I really didn't expect this to continue after you quit."

"I also didn't expect this because of how things ended last time we were here. How is everyone at the office doing?" I said, trying to change the subject.

"Exactly the same, Steve. Did you really think quitting was going to change anyone's life?"

"I thought it would at least make the office a little less interesting."

"The only less interesting part is that now Jim doesn't have you as a scapegoat, so he is being a bigger dick to everyone."

"Oh good! Now you know what I was going through. You've only had a few days with him. Try years with that guy," I said flippantly.

There was a pause in the banter. Not a big one, but big enough to raise some level of concern. I like talking, but not as much as John, and between the two of us, there is hardly ever a break; which is why we get along so well. Silence is burdensome and uncomfortable, and the longer it lingers, the harder it is to get back in the rhythm of a conversation.

"All jokes aside," John started, the smile disappearing off his face, "you need to reconsider. Talk to your father-in-law and try to get your job back. Say you'll make all the changes you didn't make before. You're going to need the money."

"For what?"

"Are you fucking delirious?" He said, slamming his fist onto the table. It was abnormal for John to take that tone with me. Actually, it's uncalled for any adult to take that tone with another without there being severe consequences. Had I not known John for as long as I did, I would have considered punching him in his already crooked nose. "Dude, your life is falling apart, and you need to wake up and grab hold of it before everything spins out of control. Don't make the mistake every other goddamn idiot makes. Nut up and go deal with your shit."

"What in the fuck are you talking about, John?"

"You need to figure your life out at some level. If you don't want to be with Linda, that's fine, but you're going to need money."

"If I don't choose to be with Linda, what do I need money for?"

John shut his eyes hard then moved his hands to his temples and started massaging them. It was a bit dramatic. Then, he reached for his beer and gulped the remaining half in about three seconds.

"Steve," John burped, "even if you decide to move on from Linda you still need money for a lot of things." He looked up from his empty glass and into my eyes. He could tell I still didn't comprehend the severity of what he was talking about. "You are going to need money to pay your rent, and bills, and be able to feed yourself and buy things like booze. Also, putting some furniture in your place probably wouldn't be a bad idea either." He hadn't broken eye contact the entire time, and it was unsettling to be staring into another person's eyes for that long. It wasn't something I was accustomed to. "Then, you're going to need to lawyer up. I'm glad you think you're taking this thing as well as you are bud, but I severely doubt Linda is doing the same."

That last sentence caught my attention, and my mind went back to the threats of her getting her father to fire me if I didn't call off the separation. Something did tell me that they would want to make me hurt. Linda and her family don't deal with things not going their way.

"Besides," John started again, "if you work the right angles you could get some alimony checks out of it. If you pay a lawyer well enough, he could get you the freedom to not work again. Linda's family is worth a fortune."

"I don't want to do that," I said.

"Then she will come after you."

"Blood from a stone," I joked.

John wanted to respond, but he didn't have a comeback for that statement. Instead, he just motioned to the bartender for two more beers. We sat there for a few moments, neither sure what we could say to break the tension that was building.

"Can I ask you something, John?" The question was clunky and awkward, but it's the best way to preface a question that potentially has significant consequences. "Did you just meet here today in hopes of convincing me to take my old job back?"

John sat back in the booth as the waitress came by and dropped the beers off. John and I had spent a lot of time in the office and drinking after hours. We had said a lot to one another, both fun and serious. I helped him when he had rough days with his ex-wife, and he would make fun of me when I complained about Linda or my job. Never, had I seen him as reticent to say something as I did right then.

"I just want you to remember there are more options than what you're entertaining right now."

"I'm not going back, John, because it's not even an option at this point. I don't mean logistically, I mean I will never even consider it."

"You're making a dumb choice."
"If that's true, at least it's mine."

10

The best part about being unemployed is the fact that you no longer need a schedule. Before quitting, or being fired, I always had to make sure I had everything mapped out to the point that I could at least lie my way through the day. For example, if I wanted to exercise I had to make sure I was up at 7:00 at the absolute latest to have time to shower and catch the 8:45 bus to get in at 9:15. I was supposed to be in at 9:00, but I could get away with it. Even if I was approached I could lie and say the bus was delayed because of the weather, or the bus driver was stung by a bee, or we were getting hit by the light rail that ran through downtown. My distraction-less bus rides gave me the time to come up with a myriad of excuses.

Today though was different. Today I woke up at 10:00 after a solid eleven hours of sleep. I felt good. No hangover and with nothing else to do, I put on my running clothes, put Vaseline all over my body to prevent chafing, and double-checked the weather. It was forty-one degrees out, still unusually warm for this late in the year.

I went outside and stretched and started on my usual running trail. I ran through the Uptown Mall, which is a small strip of nature homeless people sleep in. During the day I like to admire the dead, leafless greenery contrasted with the small piles of pure white snow. In Minnesota, the snow that falls from November on will stick around until March when it finally melts.

After the Mall, I took a left on Lake Calhoun and started to really get into my rhythm. I looked out onto the partially frozen lake and thought about summer and the times Linda and I would go canoeing. We would bring weed and a pipe to get high once we got far away from the other boats. It sounds much more fun than it was though. Linda would get too stoned and it would be my responsibility to paddle and steer us back to shore. It also didn't help that we had a cooler full of ice and beer that weighed us down. A cornerstone of any outdoor activity on a hot summer day.

Just then, a woman wearing a bright red shirt passed me on the left. I didn't get a good look at her, but she seemed like a perfect runner. She stood straight up and was comfortable, like she was gliding on the sidewalk. Although I was clearly huffing and puffing at this point, the quick look I got at her face showed that she wasn't tired and she had no intention of slowing down. She left my sight as she was running about a minute and a half faster per mile than I was and she vanished in the gentle curve of dead trees that circled the lake. Her blonde ponytail bobbing into the distance.

On days like today, the lake is teeming with people. Even though it was a Wednesday morning, there were students, night workers, the unemployed, and retirees who are lucky enough to enjoy the last good day before winter took over. All of us embracing the final gift nature would give us for months and months and months.

As I passed the, "fishing dock," as locals deemed it, I was about a quarter done with the run. Just under one mile, but I could already feel the energy seeping out of my legs. I could tell my initial confidence was wearing down, and although I thought I was hitting my stride, I wasn't even close to doing so. I could feel old injuries resurfacing, reminding me that this was no longer a well-tuned machine. My knee ached from a small ligament tear that happened while I was playing soccer a few years ago. My ankle was clicking and sore from a litany of countless sprains over my youth. From an injury at the beach as a twelve-year-old to a high ankle sprain from a trampoline when I was sixteen, to a time I rolled it as was leaving a football stadium just a few months ago, it was regularly getting injured, reinjured, and always in pain. The only way to get past it was to power through it.

As I considered stopping and catching my breath, just a few hundred yards from the fishing dock, I saw a man, undeniably a young hipster, walking his cat. I'm all for people doing what they want. After all, this is America. The only problem is that this guy would now take the eye roll I gave him, go to his neighborhood bar, order a PBR tallboy, and talk about how he has the right to walk down the busiest running trail in Minneapolis with a cat on a leash, and how he doesn't care how many dirty looks he got because he is allowed to do it.

The street goes both ways. If you can walk around with a cat on a leash, then I can look at you like you're a dick. Freedom of expression isn't just the way you think. Secretly you like my eye rolls because it's probably the only kind of attention you get.

At this point, I could tell the running was affecting me because I was in such a foul mood. Usually, I just let things like that go, but it was impossible to block the thoughts out due to my exhaustion and discomfort. My patience was at zero. Specifically for men with cats on leashes.

I rounded a corner where the true summer spot of Lake Calhoun is. There are sand pits and old, tattered nets for volleyball games, gazebos for poor family birthday parties, and stationary grills for even poorer family birthday parties. I could feel the running effects really beating me. I was wheezing and felt hot from the movement and cold from the sweat being whipped by the cool air. My brain was telling me desperately to stop, but I had to keep pushing.

The volleyball nets were hardly even behind me when I saw her. A woman was on the ground in a lazy, fetal position. I couldn't see her face, but I knew who she was the second I got close because of the bright red shirt. I could see the blonde ponytail. A small group of five to eight people were standing around her.

"Is everything ok?" I asked as I approached. More than 99% of the time you ask this question the answer is a simple, yes. I figured she was running too fast, and she had just collapsed from exhaustion.

"Somebody is driving on the running path," a man said.

Those aren't words you hear that often. It isn't that you don't understand something like this, it's just the word combination is so strange that it takes a minute for your brain to process it.

"Like a drunk person?"

"No. It looked like an old lady."

I looked at the scene around me. People were milling around, most of them on their phones, calling the police or paramedics for assistance. Others just looked at the ground uncomfortably, not sure how they could help, but also too good of people to just leave the poor injured woman behind.

"What happened?" The woman shrieked. She was in shock from the event and didn't have a solid grasp on what was happening or why.

"There was an accident," An older gentleman said taking her hand and grasping it for support.

"Why?" she wailed. She moved out of the fetal position, and it was clear there was substantial damage to not only her face but her legs as well. She was bloody and bruised with a puddle of urine quickly growing around her waist.

"The car dragged her for about 20 feet." The man next to me whispered.

And we all just stood there until the police and ambulance arrived. Some people were stopping walkers on the path, others helped flag down the police and ambulance, a few tried to comfort the woman, but mostly we just stood there. Too good to leave and too powerless to help. It was a waste of everybody's time.

After about ten minutes, she was being loaded into an ambulance and people began to wander off. Up the path, just past where it bends, and the trees start to obscure the view, you could just make out the back of a car and police lights through the sparse leaves on the grey, dying branches.

That's when I decided I should probably take a vacation.

11

"You haven't been over for family dinner in months," Mom said. She hadn't even waited for me to go to the front door before confronting me in the driveway.

"I've been swamped, Mom," I said.

"Too busy for family? Too busy for me?"

"It's not like that."

"Steven, don't talk to your mother in that tone," Dad chimed in through the open front door.

"Listen, I have just been really preoccupied with the separation, the pending divorce, I just quit my job-"

"Hold on," Mom interjected, "you didn't even *mention* that you quit your job. Are you working somewhere else? Are you having trouble paying the rent? Did Linda's father push you out because you are divorcing his daughter?"

"Calm down, Mom."

"Don't tell me to calm down!" She yelled forcefully. I saw curtains moving in the neighbor's windows after this outburst, which didn't bother me, but it clearly bothered my mother, who blushed and looked down at the ground, somewhat ashamed that she yelled at her thirty-one year-old son. Once it was clear she had been embarrassed into calming down, I figured it would be best to speak up.

"It's just been a lot of work. I don't have the time to drive out here every week anymore."

"If it's so much work, then why are you here?" She asked angrily.

"I wanted to come for dinner. I know it's not family dinner night, but I thought it would be nice to stop by."

Some of the anger started to dissipate, and she smiled. She had had a glint of admiration in her eyes. I knew my next sentence was not going to go over well.

"I also need a small favor."

Her smile instantly vanished.

"It's not a big one. I just need you to look after Jackson for a week or so."

"Who is Jackson?"

"My cat. Well, technically, Linda's cat."

"Then why doesn't Linda watch him?"

"He doesn't like her."

Mom looked up at the sky and tossed her head back and forth. She stuck her tongue into her cheek, an old habit that persisted from when we were kids. This was her 'Mom face' she would make when she was thinking about something we asked her when we were younger. Being animated for children is a good way to make them believe you're actually considering their request. Unfortunately for her, she did it so much it became a habit, and she couldn't stop doing it whenever she weighed her options.

"That depends," she said slowly regaining eye contact and recentering her tongue.

"On what?"

"On two things."

"Name them."

"The first is you need to come to more family dinners. At least two a month. I get worried when you don't come here to visit us."

This was a fair request. I had been regularly coming to family dinners for years and to suddenly stop was uncalled for. I needed to ease out of it, not just rip off the Band-Aid. It was ridiculous to assume there to be no repercussions.

"That's fine," I said.

"Second," she said as her face became more serious, "you have to try and patch things up with Linda."

This request seemed a little less fair.

"You took vows the day you got married in front of all of us that you would be with each other no matter what. I would hate to see you break that because of some ridiculous spat."

"She left me because we're not happy."

"Promise me, or I won't watch the cat."

In this instance, I really had no option. I could tell this trade had very little to do with me and my happiness, just like she didn't care about any of my siblings being happy. She didn't care that Abby had an empty life and marriage as long as she kept humbly bragging. She wasn't interested in my sister's kids destroying her marriage as long as she didn't talk about it. It wasn't that different from Sergio being continuously stoned, and potentially being interested in men. It was a strict don't ask, don't tell policy.

"Ok," I lied.

My Mom faked a smile.

Hardly Harding

FLORIDA

1

I don't care who disagrees, and I know this statement is not going to be a popular one, but drinking gin in an airport before 10 a.m. on a weekday is by far the best way to travel.

The concourse was bustling with serious businessmen. It was a Tuesday afternoon and the middle of the week isn't a big travel day for families or young coeds going on vacation. Just for the casual, unemployed man with time and money to waste. The restaurant I was sitting in was a sea of black and dark grey suits with boring, once color ties. I only had a carry on because I wasn't planning on more than a five-day stay. Also, it was an easy way to avoid the $30 fee.

Generally, when people get divorced or are in the process of it, there are a few reasonable options you get a pass with. The first is a cruise during Spring Break. Sure, you aren't 21, and even if you're one to two decades older than the average attendee, there are always a few girls with daddy issues who will sleep with you because you can buy alcohol at the bar for them and not have to take them back to your room for cheap vodka you smuggled in using water bottles. This is usually the route people go who got married way too young and need to get some partying out of their system.

The second is the spiritual journey. See *Eat, Pray, Love.* A great place to go for this is India since that is the epicenter of mental and physical reawakening. Yoga, meditation, reincarnation, the whole far east religion thing really gives westerners validation of a rebirth. Any impoverished country works, but for some reason, India is the pinnacle of coming back and being seen as changed. You can be officially baptized from your previous life and onto your next journey.

The third, most general one you can do is going to the Caribbean, Jamaica, or Mexico. If you go to Hedonism in Jamaica, you get a pass as unshackling the oppression of only sleeping with one person. You can go to Mexico or the Caribbean route of drinking yourself into oblivion and gorging on local foods. Just time spent on the beach, watching the waves; maybe a gutsy tourist will try surfing and meet a sweet local girl.

The underlying theme for all of these trips is that they are expensive, and I no longer had the luxury of booking vacations and not looking at cost.

A balding middle-aged man sat next to me at the bar. "Can I have a bottle of water please?" He pleasantly asked the bartender. We made brief eye contact and smiled. He wasn't a good-looking guy, but he wasn't ugly either. He wore a way-too-tight white shirt with a black suit, black pants, and a black tie. I was wearing a stereotypical Hawaiian shirt that was bright orange, with hibiscus flowers and leaves that were multicolored all over it. My dark blue board shorts didn't help make me look respectable, and neither did my flip-flops with bottle openers on the soles. It also made him suspicious that I was a grown man with a JanSport backpack. I could tell he was trying to figure me out.

At best I was an eccentric CEO.

Potentially, I was an unemployed stunt double for someone who wasn't even famous.

At worst, and most likely in his eyes, I was a deadbeat dad of five with four different mothers. This was also accentuated by the gin and tonic I had just feverishly finished and ordered another round of. So, I guess you could say he was leaning more towards the latter.

"Where are you heading?" I asked meekly.

The businessman perked up and looked around. He wasn't sure if I was talking to him, someone around him, or myself. After all, I was getting drunk at an airport bar, alarmingly early, and very alone, and even if this is the only socially acceptable place to drink in the morning, it still is a warning sign.

"Chicago," he replied curtly.

"Business or pleasure?" Right when these words came out of my mouth, it felt like classic bad movie dialogue.

"Some of both," he said through a grin. This was somehow an even worse line of dialogue. "What about you?"

"I'm just going on a vacation." The bartender set my drink down and swapped it for my used glass.

"Alone?"

"Yup."

"Where are you going?"

"Florida."

"It's a great time to get in some rounds of golf. You going for that?"

"Nope. Never cared for golf."

"Going for the theme parks?"

"I'm just planning on it being low key. You know, do some swimming, go to the beach, maybe a little fishing. Just unwind a little bit."

"Which city you going to?"

"I'm flying into Orlando, and just driving east toward the beach. I'll probably wind up in the Daytona Beach area."

This made the businessman wince.

"There really hasn't been much going there since the 90's. Once MTV stopped doing spring break there, the whole place kind of crumbled."

"That sounds perfect," I replied taking a big swig of gin.

"You staying anywhere nice?" He asked, trying to make more conversation.

"I haven't looked at any hotels yet," I confessed. "I don't even have a way to get from Orlando to Daytona."

The businessman laughed, and the bartender gave him his bottle of water. He thought for a second, looked at his watch, dug through his pockets and found his boarding pass. He studied it for a few seconds pondering what to do next. Then placed it into his wallet, and sat down next to me as he cracked open his water.

"Can I ask you something?" He asked.

"Sure."

"Why are you going on vacation?"

"Well, I just quit my job, my wife and I are getting a divorce, and I just need some time away."

"Yeah, I've been divorced twice. Both times I went to Vegas and met girls, gambled, got drunk, went to strip clubs." His voice trailed off as he thought of those hot desert days in Las Vegas meeting women and losing money. He smiled as he remembered all the names he had forgotten and days he had spent living like an animal, off instinct, years ago.

"Truth be told," I started, breaking him out of his daydream, "I couldn't tell you why I picked it. It just seemed like the right place to go."

"Well then, go with your gut I suppose."

A tense, awkward silence occurred while I reconsidered my decision to go to Florida, and this man got nostalgic about his post-divorce experiences.

"Good luck," he finally said getting up, grabbing the rolling bag that was behind him. He patted me on the back, and I tapped on my glass for another.

2

I was jolted awake by the plane making contact with the runway. I felt half drunk and couldn't remember very much of the airport or the flight at first. Somehow I had managed to make my way to the gate on time, which judging by the fact that I was still reasonably buzzed and not hungover was nothing short of a miracle.

I looked down at my watch. It was 6:47 p.m. I tried to piece everything together, but there was a thick mental fog preventing me from recalling too much. I remembered the conversation with the businessman and his condescending advice for me to change my plans and to go to Vegas. He left, and I continued to drink hard for the next three or four hours until I had to make my way to the terminal. I checked my pockets and found three mini bottles of vodka, one coaster with a phone number scrawled on it, and a receipt for a transaction totaling $134.98. This was for eleven gin and tonics, and one order of mozzarella sticks. That was my staple blackout food. Linda could always tell I was too drunk when I ordered them.

"Are they going to let me get my rental car?" I asked myself, sifting through my wallet to ensure I still had my ID and credit cards. "I am reasonably drunk. Is this going to pose a problem?" The fear and anxiety were creeping in as I felt the cold, gin filled sweats on my forehead. After a few minutes of weighing my options, I figured I would get away with being slightly over the limit as long as I grabbed a coffee, and talked as little as possible.

I looked next to me trying to get my bearings back. Sitting in the middle seat was a little girl, probably no older than eight, staring back at me. I smiled and nodded at her, and she giggled as she turned away and looked at her mother who seemed much less happy to see me awaken from my drunken state. She glared at me, judgmentally as the pile of small empty booze bottles and trash fell out of my lap and onto the floor. I didn't break eye contact though. This was my vacation, and I wasn't going to let some lady make me feel bad because Disney World is here too.

3

"Next," the young man said waving me down the counter. I walked in his direction, trying my best to portray myself as put together as possible. I had a half finished Starbucks coffee in my hand, and I think that made me look respectable despite my disheveled appearance.

"Hello," I said calmly, "I rented my car online." I pulled up my phone and showed him the rental confirmation page.

The man immediately put his head down and started typing. Renting the car had been my idea at the airport bar just a few hours earlier. This was before the mozzarella sticks pre-blackout. Before I was just going through the motions of being alive. I took the, "economical," option at 7 dollars a day.

"Would you like to purchase any additional insurance on your car?" He asked.

"How much is it?"

"An additional 15 dollars a day."

"No thank you."

He started typing feverishly again.

I looked around. I was the only single man in the place renting a car. In the distance, I could hear the screams of cranky children and frustrated tones of parents frantically trying to get their minivans.

Without looking up, the rental guy started, "Would you like to use our fuel up option? It is actually cheaper than the-"

"No thanks."

He went back to typing.

I turned away and looked out the window, and saw my reflection. I looked like shit. I had huge, dark bags under my eyes, which clashed with my ghostly white complexion. Even from the distance of fifteen yards away I could make out stains and blotches all over the front of my Hawaiian shirt that I had forgotten about from the airport, or the airplane, or somewhere.

Tomorrow was Wednesday. If I still worked at the office, I would have my weekly 'Purpose of Power' meeting. For me, this was a joke. However, a lot of my coworkers jumped at the opportunity to learn, "life skills." They were held on the top floor of the tower we worked in, where the CEO, President, VP of Operations, and those types all had their offices which were all often empty.

The idea behind Purpose of Power was to help comb the next group of managers. It was also a three and a half hour break from being on the floor, and actually working, so people really wanted to be in this seminar. We were supposed to talk about goals, what we wanted out of this job, and what we wanted out of life. It was all a waste of time, empowerment bullshit. At its heart, this seminar was as empty as everything else in American corporate culture. It was the equivalent of a book of quotes from Buddhist monks. It was a way to turn your life around in thirty days. It was losing ten pounds a week. It was by far, my least favorite workday. However, Jim insisted I do it to turn my attitude around.

There was one morning when a woman was openly weeping in front of other adults that she worked with. She was crying because she and her husband had poured their savings into remodeling their kitchen and she didn't like the way it came out. I remember her saying, through tears, "We dug into our retirement to complete this, and it came out the way the contractors promised, but it just didn't feel like home anymore."

She was too oblivious to see it had nothing to do with the kitchen. I'm not a licensed therapist, but it was probably because she had realized her job was a joke, or that she hated her life, or that her marriage was falling apart, or she didn't want to be a mom anymore, or something just as terrible you aren't allowed to say.

"Would you like to upgra-"

"No thank you."

The typing quickened, and the face of the rental man contorted into an uncomfortable grimace.

What was sad about these meetings wasn't the fact that people were crying about kitchens, or so desperately trying to move up the corporate ladder. It was sad because people really hadn't spent any time and questioned their choices. I'm not delusional. I know I don't have the answers, but some of these people didn't even ask themselves why they were working a corporate job or what they wanted out of life. This seminar, that rivaled the depth of a bargain bin self-help book, was the first time these 40-year-olds had reflected on any life decisions.

"I will need your ID," he said.

I put my coffee down and got my driver's license out of the plastic sleeve, and handed it to him.

He didn't even look up to confirm it was me.

"Alllllll riiiiiight," he said slowly without looking up. He handed me the keys and pointed out the door. "Your car will be in the fifth row to the right outside the doors.

"Thank y-"

"NEXT," he shouted at nobody behind me.

4

I walked out of the car rental office and out into the hot, sticky air. This was my first time outside in Florida, and I could understand the stereotypes of the state already. It was like stepping into a swamp. For me, it felt harder to breathe, like I was inhaling over a bowl of hot soup. I needed the rain to come and wash away the humidity and heat and relieve some of this unbearable, thick air.

I wandered five rows down and came to the "economical" cars section. They weren't junk cars, they were just outrageously small. They reminded me of the vehicles Europeans drive. Compact and reasonable but lacking the bulk Americans are so fond of. I pressed the lock button on my keys and a few rows down, a white Mitsubishi Mirage that was just a few years old, blinked its headlights.

Once I got to the car, I threw my bag inside and sat down in the driver seat. I adjusted the mirrors and started the engine. I blasted the air conditioning and let it cool me down. I already had beads of sweat rolling down my face just from my brief time outside. For a few minutes I sat there, thinking back to Purpose of Power and that woman crying about her wasted money and subpar kitchen. In that moment, I realized Linda wasn't that different. Maybe she wouldn't cry in front of coworkers, but she could never see the forest through all the trees. It wasn't that she didn't like hanging out with her friends, it was just that they always picked the wrong place to do it. The restaurant had terrible food, or Christina wouldn't stop talking about her husband, or the music was lousy, or the bar was too loud, or the drinks were too expensive. Excuse, after excuse, after excuse. Then again, maybe my way of dealing with things isn't the most direct or healthy either.

5

The drive took closer to an hour and forty-five minutes because I got lost several times due to some dead zones on the freeways. It didn't help that driving the speed limit in Florida seemed like a death sentence, especially in a car as small as mine. Most of the vehicles on the highway were trucks or SUVs that would have blasted my rear bumper all the way to the driver seat. In addition to this, there were numerous old people driving way under the speed limit in the right lane, and drunk rednecks driving way over the speed limit in the left lane. It was a melting pot of chaos and confusion, of recklessness and dementia, that only a true native could understand.

I pulled into The Desert Inn after the sun had set. The neon sign illuminated the parking lot, and the 'Vacancy' sign was missing all of the 'a' and 'c' letters. Underneath the 'V   n y" sign was the hotel marquee which read, "Special! 39 dollars a nights!" When I had booked it online in my gin filled state, it was twenty-five dollars a, "nights," and I figured that just like the outdated red and yellow neon sign, the marquee hadn't been updated in a while either.

I parked in the nearly empty lot, grabbed my backpack out of the front seatand walked into the lobby. I wasn't sure what to expect exactly, but I was surprised at what the inside looked like. I don't want to say it was a bad hotel, because that really wouldn't be fair. It looked like at one time this place was very modern. It was just that it was modern about forty-five years ago and no updates had been made to it since.

When I say no updates, I mean absolutely no updates. The carpet looked like it had been given up on, as it was covered in sand and various stains of different colored alcohols. As I scanned the lobby, I noticed there was an old bar to my right. It would have been a neat, retro looking place to grab a beer. It had a brass rail, a thick wooden top, and one of those large Guinness mirrors behind the booze in an attempt to class up the place. But the entire bar had been converted into storage, and boxes were stacked up to the taps. All of this was covered in thick, filmy dust, that made me think before they could open it back up they would need to pass several thorough inspections.

On the plus side, there was a vintage chandelier in the lobby, and the check-in desk looked like something out of a black and white movie. They had those wooden slots behind the counter where they kept rooms' skeleton keys, mail, or whatever else a receptionist would throw into it. The counter itself was a white marble that was a high-class staple of the hotel for decades. I'm sure years ago this place was frequented by high-class businessmen.

But now this place was a hunk of shit.

Not only was this place old, but it was also seemingly abandoned by both the people staying here and the employees. I still hadn't seen one person in the hotel anywhere. There wasn't a custodian, or a bellhop, a concierge, or a receptionist in sight.

After a few minutes, I rang the small bell on the desk, and a sixteen year-old girl came walking out of the backroom. She didn't look up from her phone as she opened the door.

"Name?" She asked, still entranced by her phone.

"Steve Harding." My voice echoed into the lobby. "Are you not expecting very many other guests tonight?" I asked sarcastically.

She rolled her eyes not even acknowledging my question and smacked her gum as she set down her phone. This was apparently some sort of inconvenience and one that she was not used to, especially at this hour. I could hear the tapping of keys and the numerous exhausted sighs from her as she looked for my reservation.

She reached seemingly at random behind her and grabbed a set of keys from the boxes behind the desk. She slammed them on the counter between us.

"Ok, you're in room 1309."

"I thought hotels weren't supposed to have a thirteenth floor," I replied in an attempt to make conversation.

"Well, we have more than thirteen floors," she said calmly. "So, we would need a thirteenth floor."

With that, she grabbed her phone off the counter, turned around, and headed into the back room.

I was alone again.

After standing at the counter for a few moments collecting myself, I went to the elevators that were in plain view of the desk, and made my way past the brochures of what to do in the area and pressed the elevator button. The light above the far right elevator blinked and made a soft dinging sound. When the doors opened up, I figured I had made some sort of mistake because it appeared to be more of a utility elevator. It was large and draped in blue tarps. After a few seconds, I realized I wasn't going to take thirteen flights of stairs and took my chances with the elevator. I went in and pressed the thirteen button and waited for a while as the doors closed, and I slowly made my ascent.

I didn't know exactly what I was expecting, but as the doors opened, it revealed something out of a horror film. The hallway was dimly lit, with an alarming number of overhead fixtures flickering or entirely out. From what I could see in the hall, it was littered with trash and old beer bottles. I couldn't tell the pattern on the carpet because of the mix of the poor lighting and the numerous food and alcohol stains that permeated everywhere.

I walked out of the elevator and came to my room a few doors down from where I was. I pulled out my keys and exhaled as I slid them into the lock; it clicked loudly, and I pushed the door open and stuck my hand inside feeling for the light switch. I heard a distant door open and footsteps coming toward me. I panicked and stumbled into the darkness to avoid meeting anyone.

The door shut behind me with a thud and I continued to run my hands along the wall, frantically looking for a switch. I was washed in total blackness and fear began to grip me. I don't know why. I'm not afraid of the dark. I just felt uneasy in the Desert Inn and needed to make sure there wasn't someone already in my room, waiting to attack me. I found the switch and without hesitation flicked it on.

After a few seconds, my eyes adjusted and I realized that I was standing in a surprisingly up to date and well-maintained room. An off-brand TV was hung on the wall, and while the furniture was cheap, it was still new. The bed was made with thick, but stainless sheets and the walls had no smudges on them.

I suppose that since I hadn't seen anyone else at the hotel yet, this could be the only one they had actually updated. It was entirely possible that the remaining units were a dilapidated mess. Each with a pile of mattresses in the middle of the floor stained with some old hooker's blood, and cigarette burns all over the carpet.

I put my bag down and went over to the window to get a good look at the ocean. It was dark out, but even with the window closed, I could hear the waves breaking on the shore not far off. I wanted to open the window so I could smell the salty air and feel the soft ocean breeze. I looked for the latch on the window along with the edges, but I couldn't see one. I then moved to the sliding glass door and searched for the hinge to unlock it, but even after finding and toying with it, it wouldn't slide open either.

"I wonder what Linda is doing tonight," I said aloud. I stopped trying to get everything open because this genuinely surprised me. I rarely talk out loud to myself, and I don't think about Linda very often.

"Knowing her," I started again, "she's probably just sitting at home, re-watching some shitty Netflix show." I inhaled deeply, and I pulled on the sliding glass door with all my might, but it wouldn't budge.

"FUCK!" I yelled.

'What if she's not at home though?' I thought. 'What if she is out getting over you? What if you haven't thought this whole thing through clearly?' I walked away from the glass door; the fury growing inside my stomach as I stomped over to the mini-fridge and opened it up. Inside it were some sodas, light beers, and mini-bottles. I carelessly grabbed one of the beers without reading it, and a small bottle of Jack Daniels. I took the shot and washed it down with the fresh, watery beer.

'Are you sure you can afford what I'm sure is an additional thirty dollars on your tab? You quit your job, you have a diminishing bank account, and you're going through a divorce. Shouldn't all of this push you toward saving the small of amount of money you have?'

I saw my reflection in the glass and my anger turned back toward the window and the jammed door. I tried to open both over and over again every way I could think of, from every imaginable angle. All the while I could feel frustration boiling inside me, and just before the breaking point of smashing all the glass in the hotel room, I called the front desk.

It took three separate calls for the girl at the front to answer, in a distant and aggravated tone, "Hello?"

"Yes, I just checked in, and there doesn't seem to be a way to open my window or get out on my balcony."

"Yeah, they don't let any hotel have doors or windows open up to the beach."

"Why?" I asked.

"Why, what?"

"Why can't I open up the windows and doors to the balcony?"

"They told me originally it had something to do with turtles laying their eggs," she said as her cell phone chimed in the background.

"What does that have to do with me opening my window?"

"I don't know. It's just a rule. Maybe it has to do with suicide or something?"

The line went silent for a few seconds.

"Thanks," I finally said.

"No problem," she hung up, and the room was silent except for the distant sound of muffled waves crashing onto the shore outside, and a rhythmic pulse thumping in my head.

I considered unplugging the phone and breaking the sliding glass door and just going out to my balcony, but it felt like too much trouble. I laid down, turned off the light and fell asleep almost immediately.

6

I woke up to the sound of motorcycles spitting and spewing down the beach. I rolled over and saw it was 10:14, and if I was going to get the most out of this vacation, I really needed to get outside and unwind. I stretched and realized I was wearing my jeans and Hawaiian shirt from the night before, and both reeked of cheap airport gin and sweat. My backpack still stood, unopened near the door, and I could feel the plaque growing on my teeth.

I made my way to the coffee maker and started to brew a pot in the hopes it would energize me out of this funk I was in. I peered out my window and saw the group of bikers making their way north, towards a pier. It didn't look very far. It was probably a little over a mile, but the exercise would help me sweat out the hangover. I knew if I didn't start moving now, I would be stuck in this room for the entire day.

I put on a different Hawaiian shirt, poured my coffee and made my way to the elevator. I pushed the down button and seconds later the doors opened to reveal two of the most stereotypical, caricature bros you can imagine. Both had on board shorts and bright orange and yellow tank tops, which by themselves didn't necessarily make them look like douchebags. It was the combination of body spray, backward hats, and sunglasses on in the elevator that really made me think these two were going to be a joy to be with in a tight space. Another off-putting fact was these guys were probably in their mid-thirties and should have grown out of this style by age nineteen.

I walked in and saw the, "L," was already lit up and kept my back to the two adults, as they carried on their conversation, hardly even noticing that I had entered the elevator.

"Dude, did you see Shawna last night?"

"Bro, I didn't know she got divorced."

"I've wanted to get in that since high school."

"I'd be careful bro. She has been married to Tyler since he knocked her up senior year."

"So?"

"So? What do you mean, 'So?' he will beat your ass if you fuck his son's mom."

"He won't do shit. The only thing he has done since the tenth grade is sell weed, and the guy is constantly baked. Trust me, he probably doesn't even realize his wife left him yet. Besides, Tyler isn't in the same shape he was in high school."

"He used to be built like a brick house!" Bro number one exclaimed.

"Now he's built like a shit house," the two said in unison as they high-fived.

The bell rang for the lobby, interrupting their loud, stoned laughs. Generally, walking out of an elevator is a social cue to quiet down and stop talking, but this didn't prevent these two from being just as loud. I promptly exited the elevator, went down the hall, and opened the heavy glass doors to the beach.

As I walked down onto the soft sand with the pier in the distance, the whole situation kept replaying in my head. It was like those two were stuck in some sort of time warp. The world around them moved away from the 90's, but they were unable to because it was all they knew. Like they had forgotten how to progress since high school. They were going to be painting houses and mowing lawns with sixteen-year-olds who are just like them until they die in what I assume will be a DUI related accident.

7

The boardwalk was a dump. A proper forgotten shithole. It had a really stabby vibe to it, and I put my sandals back on once I got closer to it out of fear of stepping on a hypodermic needle. I'm not a neat freak, but the entire pier looked like there hadn't been any upkeep since the early 80's. I passed an arcade, an open-air shop where a guy was airbrushing T-shirts and license plates, a small go-cart track, and a cheap beach store that had towels and sunscreen for sale. All of this was just on the land that was around the boardwalk itself, and the actual pier only had some fishermen and a Joe's Crab Shack. The juxtaposition of the two didn't really make a lot of sense, and I figured people eating seafood wouldn't really want to see fisherman catching their dinner alive. You would never put a steakhouse next to a slaughterhouse. It's too macabre. Regardless, the place was packed with both the poor catching dinner and the rich on vacation, eating frozen meals of what was freshly caught next to them.

Luckily, in the midst of all of the head shops, heroin addicts, and unattended children running out of the arcade, there was a bar at the far end of everything. It was a slushie bar that had a line of machines all swirling cold flavored ice. I walked up confidently and sat down on one of the stools that was bolted to the ground. The whole place was covered by a thin tarp, and the sun pierced through many of the holes, providing little protection.

"I'll have a Daiquiri," I said to the bartender.

She turned around and without looking up replied in a low, raspy voice, "We ran out of Daiquiri."

When I got a good look at her face. She was old, but she was definitely younger than she looked. There were years of hard living behind the wrinkles and the nicotine-stained teeth.

"How about a Margarita then?"

"We don't have that here," she said.

"How about a Piña Colada?"

Without responding, she grabbed a cup, turned around, and pulled a lever. Slush nearly overflowed to the lip of the plastic rim. Without looking, she switched it back and started pouring rum in with the mix and stirred it with a straw. She hastily threw it down on the bar, but amazingly didn't spill a drop. The whole thing took less than ten seconds.

"That'll be $9.50," she said, not even looking at me

I gave her my credit card and started to drink. I turned around in my stool and looked out onto the crashing waves. I could hear them better than I could see them. There wasn't a cloud in the sky, making the beach impossible to see through the glare of the ocean and sand. I looked down at the cup, and it read in big bold letters:

BIKE WEEK 2007

"Do they have Margaritas?" A timid voice asked.

I turned to my right and saw a young woman, in her early twenties, sitting in the seat next to mine. I hadn't heard anyone walking near me, nor did I hear the soft sound of a person sitting next to me. She had almost just appeared.

She was blonde, with blue eyes, and she had a warm smile. She wasn't breathtakingly gorgeous or dressed like the other women on the beach. There was just something about her; a youthful glow that hadn't been beaten out of her yet.

"No," I replied.

"What about Daiquiris?"

"Not those either."

"What did you get?"

"Just a Piña Colada."

"I'll have one of those too," she said, smiling at the old woman.

We sat for a second in silence. I wasn't sure what exactly to say to her. I also was out of the dating game for so long, I couldn't tell if she was buying herself a drink on my tab, or if she was just being polite and sitting next to me.

"I'm Nikki," she said putting out her hand.

"I'm Steve," I replied, shaking her hand firmly. "Are you on vacation?" I tried to make quick conversation since this was the first person to talk to me since the middle-aged man recommended Vegas to me at the airport.

"Sort of," she replied.

"How are you 'sort of' on vacation?"

"Well, it's supposed to be," she said this while turning her head behind her, looking at the ocean. I may have been out of the game for a long time, but I knew that if I wanted her to stay, I needed to change the subject.

"We don't have to talk about-"

"My husband," she interrupted, "he has been off doing a lot of things this trip." She looked more intensely at the ocean and pretended to watch the crashing waves through the blinding sun.

"That's ok," I said enthusiastically. "There will be more trips. I did something similar with my wife with our last trip to Denver. She wanted to go hiking and horseback riding, but I just wanted to get high and eat at the local restaurants."

Nikki laughed, but it was laughter that thinly veiled melancholy.

The old woman put the Piña Colada down, and although Nikki reached for her back pocket to pay for, I motioned for her to put in on my tab.

"You didn't have to do that," she said in a surly tone.

"Consider it a wedding gift."

She laughed again and smiled at me.

"I'm sure whatever your husband did, it was an accident. Really, you have a lifetime of trips ahead of you."

"Yeah," she started, "he just he keeps playing golf, and he's treating this like a chance to see all of his old fraternity brothers again." She deeply exhaled and took a big swig of her drink. Her face twisted suddenly, and it contorted as she scrunched her cheeks and eyes together.

"Brain freeze?"

She smiled again after a few moments of silence, nodding and confirming my question. Her face shifted back to normal, and she said, "It's just our honeymoon. This isn't the way I dreamt it would be. I thought it would be swim-up bars, and excursions together. Not just me, alone wandering boardwalks, drinking with strangers."

"I know what you mean. Marriage can be trying and difficult," I confessed in a solemn tone. "I should have clarified that technically my 'wife' is my soon to be ex-wife."

Nikki's cocked her head to the side, and that brain freeze face came back. "Are you serious? Are you coming onto me right now?"

"What? No?!"

"I'm on my honeymoon, and you're telling me you came on a trip down here to Florida to get laid?"

"It's not like that at all. Please, let me explain-"

She was already taking a drink of her Piña Colada and giggling to herself.

"You're fucking with me right now? Are you serious?"

"I couldn't resist," she replied through laughter.

"Well, while I can't say my wife was out playing golf during our honeymoon, I can say that things in my marriage didn't turn out exactly the way I expected."

"Are you saying me and Matt are getting a divorce?"

"Of course not! What I'm saying is sometimes you really have to evaluate if this is worth throwing a marriage away over. And, while I don't know you very well, I doubt you would do that over something so petty. I'm sure your husband will get a stern talking to, but divorce seems extreme to say the least."

Nikki smiled. Her face was brightening, and there was a shimmer of hope in her eyes that were distant only a few minutes before. I think she was just happy to hear someone in her corner. We sat there, unsure what to say until she broke our silence and asked, "Can I ask you something personal?"

"Of course."

"Well, what happened that was worth throwing *your* marriage away?"

I winced at the question.

"We don't have to talk about it if you don't want."

"It's ok. I haven't talked about it at all really, and I don't know you, so I feel pretty comfortable." I looked down at my Piña Colada and noticed the slush was turning into water in the relentless sun. I took a big gulp of it, and some of it fell onto my shirt and into my lap. "You're also the first person to ask me that."

"Really?"

"Well, people ask you, and you have a standard line you deliver. Something like 'we were fighting all the time' or 'I just haven't been happy for a while.'"

"Are those things true?"

"They're true, but it wasn't why it ended."

Nikki leaned forward in anticipation. Her eyes were wide and curious as I mulled over how to explain it. I liked seeing her realize that marital problems weren't something rare or even uncommon.

"It wasn't one thing with Linda and me."

"Your ex-wife?"

"Yeah," I said, realizing I hadn't said her name yet. "It was a gradual process. One thing after another just added up."

Nikki stared at me, confused about what I was trying to say.

"It was almost like we were on two boats out on a lake and we weren't paying attention to each other. Initially, we were just a little separated, and we thought it wasn't a big deal. But then we slowly, almost unnoticeably, began to drift apart. Even when it started, I didn't think it was a problem, because she was right there. I could still throw a rope to tie us up, but I didn't because I thought I could always do it later. After years and years of gradual shifts of wind and currents we were at the other sides of the lake before we even realized it."

"Did you just come up with that?"

"No," I confessed, taking another swig of my drink, "our therapist used it on one of our last sessions together."

Nikki started laughing and involuntarily and spit some of her drink onto my face. This of course only encouraged her to laugh more, and she spit even more of her Piña Colada onto the bar.

"I'm sorry," she said laughing, "that's the saddest thing I've ever heard."

The two couples around us sharing a morning cocktail suddenly got their things and left.

"Do you think they left because of you?" I asked sarcastically.

"I'm going to have to ask you to leave," the old woman behind the bar said sternly. "I can't have you guys throwing up on the counter and sticking around." She laid my credit card and the charge for two drinks on the spit up Piña Colada.

"I probably better get back to my hotel anyways," Nikki hesitantly said. "While I don't think anyone will be there, I should still be around in case Matt comes back." For a few seconds, we both sat there, not knowing what to say. "It was really nice meeting you." She finally blurted out.

"I don't mean to be too forward with you Nikki, but I had a lot of fun talking and hanging out. We should see each other again."

Nikki looked at me quizzically. I understood this was an odd request, and she seemed to know that I was smart enough to realize that. However, this was an unusual situation and one that warranted a little extra thought. After all, a newly divorced man hanging out with a newlywed does, objectively, seem problematic. At the same time, who golfs so much on their honeymoon to even let something like this happen?

"Why not?" She said flippantly. "At the very least you might make my husband jealous, and then he'll actually spend some time with me."

I laughed, and she wrote her number down on the receipt. She smiled at me while she handed it over as she got up and walked the opposite way of my hotel. I watched her for a while, and eventually, she turned around, smiled, and waved at me, right before she disappeared into a crowd of other tourists coming out of a t-shirt shop.

8

The ring and rattle of the hotel room phone tore into the silence and abruptly shook me from a deep sleep into a foggy hangover. I had bought a case of beer and a few bottles of wine from a sketchy liquor store down the street so I could drink without raiding the mini-fridge. It had been a long day since I saw Nikki, but nothing else had happened. I was just drinking, alone, watching the sunset through my sealed window. People tell you all the time to make sure not to drink alone, but drinking alone is the best way to do it. Nobody to talk to, nobody bothering you, no endless stories about people's kids, where they went to school, or the time they met a celebrity. Just that still, stale air and a room filled with empty beer cans and nearly every surface covered in wine ring stains.

I picked up the receiver but didn't say anything into it.

"Hello?" I heard from the other end.

"Yes?" I replied.

"Steven? This is your mother."

I turned over, and on cue, the chord from the telephone knocked down the pyramid of beer cans on the nightstand along with the empty bottle of wine. It was a carpeted hotel room floor, so nothing shattered, but it was still loud enough of a crash to make me wince.

"Are you drinking?"

"What do you want, Mom?"

"I'm just calling to check in and see how your vacation is going. You won't answer your cell phone, so I thought I'd try your hotel."

"How did you know where I'm staying?"

"Linda told me."

"How does Linda know?"

"I don't know, Steven," she replied. "She is your wife, why don't you call and ask her?" This was followed by a long silence.

"Why are you calling me, Mom?"

"Well, since you brought it up," Mom said in a snappy tone, "I saw Linda tonight."

"Great."

"She was out on a date."

"Fine."

"That's all you have to say?" I could hear my Mom's tone growing more agitated. I hadn't heard her talk to me like this since I was a kid, and even through my headache, I could remember the last time she had. I had got caught cheating on a spelling test in school, and she had given me a lecture on the importance of education, and how cheaters never actually get anywhere. The word was, "clergyman."

"Yes," I replied, "I don't care, Mom."

"Steven, call her now. Call her and get her back. This temper tantrum has gone on long enough. You promised you would. Call her and piece this whole mess together."

"Ok."

"Really?"

"Yes, I'll call her now."

"That's fantastic!"

"I love you, Mom."

"I love you too, son."

"I gotta go Mom. I have to fix my marriage."

"I'm so proud of you Steven. Goodbye."

"Goodbye, Mom," I said as I hung up the phone.

I went to the bathroom sink where I was chilling my beers with ice from the night before. I cracked one open and shook the foam off my hands. I took a few sips of the warming, skunked beer and looked at myself in the mirror. I didn't like what I saw.

I walked back to the nightstand and made my way around the empty cans and wine bottle and picked up the receiver. I knew what I had to do.

The phone rang over and over again.

"Front desk," an unenthusiastic voice said.

"Hello, this is Steve Harding in room 1309. I would appreciate it if you would hold my calls."

"For how long?"

"The entire time I'm here please."

"No problem." She briskly hung up.

Even after the harsh talk my Mom gave to me years ago, I still cheated my way through middle and high school. Unsurprisingly, I cheated my way through college too. Because, ultimately, doing things untraditionally and full of dishonesty might not be the best way, but it is the most efficient. If I only felt bad about myself after talking to Mom, then I wouldn't speak to her.

9

"You look like shit!" Nikki said as she approached the table.

"Thanks, Nikki," I said softly.

"How hungover are you?" The joking had stopped, and she was now genuinely concerned about me.

"Very," I replied curtly. "I need some coffee and toast, or I might literally die." She giggled at this, and I even managed to laugh through the pain.

"I haven't seen a case this bad since I was in college," she said, concern creeping back into her voice.

"It was a long night."

My phone vibrated in my pocket, and I took it out and saw it was Mom. I had three missed calls from her and one from Linda this morning. I also had numerous unread text messages that numbered well into the double digits.

"You too important for me now?" Nikki said, annoyed.

"I'm just getting harassed."

"By who? You're divorced."

"Soon to be divorced."

"Still, who is bothering you?"

"Just my soon to be ex-wife and Mom."

"This is the least sexy conversation I've ever had."

I turned off my phone and Nikki grinned.

"What about your husband?" I asked trying to change the subject.

"What about him?"

"Well, it's not like I'm complaining about it, it's just we're just hanging out again on your honeymoon."

Nikki reached into her purse and took out a pack of menthol cigarettes, and lit it using the candle in the middle of the table.

"Can I have one of those?" I asked.

"I didn't know you smoked."

"I don't very often, but they do seem to help my hangovers."

She handed me a Newport. I took her's out of her mouth and lit mine, inhaling deeply to get it going.

A voice suddenly and sternly said from behind me, "I'm sorry, sir and ma'am, but you cannot smoke out here."

"We're outside," I said indignantly.

"It's still a health hazard, sir," the man sneered.

"We're literally the only people here," Nikki replied, motioning to the empty tables around us.

"I will be calling the police if you don't put those out."

Nikki and I looked at each other, and without saying a word, we stood up and made our way toward the beach.

Once we were about fifteen feet from the table the waiter, who was surprised by our reaction yelled out, "Fine! I never want to see you back here again." The threat didn't come off as intended because his voice had cracked and we didn't care. This wasn't either one of our hotel's restaurants, so we had no stake in being banned for life. All we both had to do was avoid the restaurant for another 5 days maximum, and we'd be fine. What was worse was now the waiter, who was already serving no tables, would now finish his shift with no tip money. His actions hurt him way more than they could ever have affected us, but you can't make a man make good choices.

We walked toward the water, smoking and not saying anything until the rolling waves and incoming tide washed cool water against our feet. We finished our cigarettes and carelessly flicked them into the surf.

"Is Florida everything you dreamed it would be?" Nikki asked, breaking the silence.

"I guess."

"Well, what did you expect here?"

"I really had no expectations. The only thing I wanted was to spend some time away from everything. Up in Minnesota, everything can get so complex with all the moving parts. Being away from it all will hopefully help me."

"Is that happening yet?"

"Not really. I don't feel any different. I don't feel away from anything."

We both stood there. Not sure what else to say.

"Have you noticed all the hookers around here?" She said trying to change the subject.

"Yeah, I've noticed them," I said, confused where she was going with this.

"What do you think they do during the day?"

"Drugs probably."

"I'm serious! Do you think they come to the beach like this?"

"Maybe some of them. Why are you asking this?"

"I'm just wondering what people who live here do. You know? What do they do with their time off?"

"Why don't you ask one?"

"Because the answer is probably drugs. I like to have the fantasy that it is something different."

10

The sound of the bells and bumpers on the pinball machine drowned out Nikki as she was talking about her husband. Since leaving the hotel restaurant and making our way to the boardwalk after stopping for some coffee and doughnuts, we were in the old arcade playing pinball and drinking. The only thing that will cure a hangover more than cigarettes is beer, and that day Nikki and I needed it for different reasons. Another day on the honeymoon meant another day Matt was out playing golf and not coming home until late because he was out with his buddies. She knew I wasn't giving her my full attention, but she didn't mind. Just half paying attention was more than she was getting without me and she couldn't really be picky at this point.

"Can I ask you a question?" I asked as my third ball went right between the flippers. She was mid-sentence, but stopped, recollected herself, and nodded. "Why did you marry this guy?"

She looked back at me, surprised I asked. After all the time we spent together, I wasn't pushing her to explain anything to me about Matt or their relationship, or what was going on. I joked about it occasionally, and we would take jabs at each other, but I hadn't been this direct so far.

"I married him because I love him," she said after a long pause.

"So?"

"So, we have been together for five years, and that's what people do. They get married after they have been together a long time." I could see she was starting to uncomfortably shift her weight back and forth and she took a huge gulp out of her beer. "I know I've painted him in a negative light, but he's not a bad guy. He's just an asshole sometimes."

Some kids ran by, interrupting her thought process and she took another sip.

"You know how I told you that I was like your husband on vacations? Being dumb? Not paying attention to my wife?"

Nikki nodded, drinking more and not looking up from her plastic cup.

"That's not true. I was the one often in your shoes."

Nikki looked up at me, and we made eye contact for a few seconds. Her blue eyes welling up with tears.

"I know how hard this is," I said, trying to soothe her.

"Excuse me," she said solemnly, "I need to use the restroom."

"Take your time," I said as I put my hand on her shoulder.

She stood there for a few seconds, enjoying the comfort, and then I wiped the tears from her eyes. She turned away and wandered into the arcade to look for the bathroom. I signaled for the waitress to bring me another beer and I put another quarter into the machine and started playing Addams Family Pinball again. My phone vibrated in my pocket, and I ignored it. Even though originally I had been the Nikki and Linda had been Matt, we had switched roles, and I was the one ignoring my wife. I was far from innocent. I was vacationing as I let it all burn in Minnesota. At that moment, as the bells rang and the lights flashed, I understood why Linda and Matt would abandon their responsibilities.

11

We had left the arcade after Nikki came out of the bathroom. The sun was setting, and we sat in Nikki's hotel lobby, drinking cheap light beer and trying to come up with what to talk about. I could see in her eyes she was in desperation mode. Now it was almost dusk so her husband couldn't be golfing, so realistically, what could he be doing that would be better than their honeymoon? She was just trying to talk about anything to get her mind off those bigger questions and wanted to spend time talking shop with a temporary friend she had made at the beach.

"Oh, childhood! We haven't talked about that."

"I didn't really have an interesting childhood. To tell you the truth, I could probably only tell you five or so stories if I tried that weren't about me getting yelled at."

"Jesus, ok. Well, that's a place to start," Nikki said, scared what would come next.

"You want to hear boring stories about when I was a kid?"

"I doubt they'd be boring. Besides, even if they are, what do you have to lose? You don't know me. You probably won't see me after this vacation. Why not? I can be your armchair psychologist."

"This sounds a little too serious."

"Fine, just tell me a few of your good ones, and I'll keep my opinions to myself. Besides, what else are we going to talk about? Your ex-wife? My husband? Let's get weird."

We laughed, and I tried to think back.

"Well, my earliest memory is my Grandma and I standing in her front yard, and it was really early in the morning."

"What were you doing?"

"We were in her garden, and she was checking this ceramic frog she had filled with beer."

"Why?"

"Slugs like beer. If you put a pan or a small bowl, or in her case, a ceramic frog out with beer in it, the slugs will crawl into it and drown as opposed to eating your plants."

"Jesus! Why were you two there?"

"We were going to salt the slugs."

"What does that do?"

"Dries them out. They just die of dehydration."

"This is not what I was expecting," Nikki said.

"So, we're standing out there, and grandma is salting the slugs, and then she hands the salt shaker to me, and motions for me to salt one too."

"So?"

"So, I cried and went inside."

"What did your grandma do?"

"Nothing. But she was old school Italian. I'm sure she judged me. After that, she wouldn't take me out into the garden and just got my brother to go with her."

"Do you have a story that is a little less depressing?" She asked.

"I mean, when I was in T-ball, my Dad and I were doing batting practice in the backyard and I hit a ball so hard that my Dad couldn't protect himself in time. It left a red spot on his stomach. That was pretty funny."

"It's unbelievable that your childhood trauma stories are just as uninteresting as your real life."

"Fine then, Nikki, what disappointing childhood stories do you have?"

"My Dad opened my college acceptance letter."

"Lame. I want you to go younger than seventeen."

"Fine, shit," she said looking up and thinking about her childhood. "Oh, my second-grade teacher, Ms. Dubois, convinced my sister to be a vegetarian."

"What's wrong with that?"

"Well, my sister and I had the same second-grade teacher, but when I was in the second grade, she was like twenty."

"Oh, wow. A real tenured teacher."

"Anyways, my sister shows up at school to pick me up one day and starts talking to Ms. Dubois about how much of an inspiration she was, and how she still hasn't touched meat since she was in her class, blah, blah blah."

"What happened?"

"Halfway through the conversation, Ms. Dubois takes a pulled pork sandwich out of her lunch box and starts putting barbecue sauce on it."

"What did your sister say?"

"She just stood there for a while. In shocked silence, and without saying anything else, left the school and never came back for anything. That day, I saw someone's entire identity crumble. Granted, it was a stupid thing to base your principles on, and as much as I want to make fun of her, she was trying to do the right thing."

"I remember being a goalie for my soccer team, and just walking off the field because my teammates were being such dicks."

"How old were you?"

"Eleven? Something like that."

"Well, at least you quit while you were ahead."

"No, then I had to get lectured all the way home about how you never give up, and how no matter how tough it is you never let your team down, all that horseshit they try and tell kids is important about sports."

"You know what I like about your stories, Steve? You did what you wanted to do. Even if everyone else thought you were wrong, you did what you thought was the right thing."

"What's that have to do with giving my Dad a bruise from a t-ball?"

"Well, that one is a wildcard. Still, the rest are you doing what you thought was the right thing."

"You know what I liked about yours? They were unbelievably sad, and made me feel better about my terrible childhood."

"Fuck you, Steve," she said hitting me across the table.

We laughed for a while, and our eyes drifted back to the setting sun. Far in the distance, I saw a white lightning bolt strike and just a few seconds later a percussive 'boom' shook both of us, and we both gasped at how deeply it had rattled us.

"You know what I don't like about your stories, Nikki?" I asked.

She silently shook her head.

"You seem like you're always in the wrong place at the wrong time, and if you are in the right place, someone else is fucking everything up."

Nikki laughed just as another loud thunderous clap rolled in from the ocean.

12

I woke up with a splitting headache to the sound of rain coming down hard just like it did every afternoon. Around noon the sky would open up and water would wash away the cigarette butts and beer caps into small streams that led to the ocean. I went over to my makeshift cooler sink and opened up another beer just in time to watch a lightning bolt strike in the distance. A warm stillness came over me for a few seconds until the deep rumble and clap of the thunder shook the ground and window. The lightning was close. Closer than the others that would roll through at this time.

The problem with a beach vacation is every time it rains, or the weather isn't what you want it to be there aren't a lot of other options for things to do. I guess I could go to the movies, or finally call Mom or Linda back, but that contradicted the whole point of this adventure. The only reason I was here was to relax and to try and get over my divorce, not reconcile a marriage. Nikki was helping a lot. Anybody at this point was helpful because I was lonely. Conversely, I don't think I was helping her very much. The more we talked, the more it seemed like she was giving up on Matt, which was the opposite of what I wanted her to do.

I went over to the bed and opened up my laptop. It was time I checked to see how much money I had left in my account. Since quitting my job, I paid off all my credit cards, and I made sure I was only using my debit card or cash. The reason was that I know how disastrously you can spend when you're on a bender.

I logged in, and the page refreshed showing my savings account totaling $472.13. I rarely touched it anyways, and this wasn't a surprise. My checking account read $313.56. This was surprising. I was sure I had over $1500 in there and to have under a quarter of that was troublesome. I checked my recent transactions and noticed that there was cash coming out from ATMs in Minneapolis. Linda was taking money. Not a lot at a time, $40, here or there, and then over the last few days the amount was increasing. She was stealing from me, and there was nothing I could do because we were still married and this was, technically, a joint account.

Even though I was trying my best to move on she wouldn't let me. Nobody would let me. Everyone was holding onto a dream that nobody wanted. Linda didn't want to be married to me. Her family didn't like me. My career was a nightmare. I couldn't understand why everyone was grasping so hard at all of this.

That's when I saw an intense white flash, followed by a loud clap, and immediately my lights went out. I looked up through my window and saw every hotels' lights out as well. Even the street lights went dark. I stood there for a minute and let the silence wash over me. The lights didn't come back on, and I started to hear curious patrons of the hotel open their doors in confusion. After just a few minutes of the room having no air circulation from either the fan or the air conditioning, and the inability to crack a window made it clear that even staying in this room for a short time wasn't going to be a possibility. I picked up my phone and called Nikki, hoping her much classier hotel wasn't in the same state of blackout mine was in.

13

"How much longer you got left?" I asked Nikki as she went to crank up the A.C.

"Just another few days. You?"

"Same." I looked around her hotel room as she fiddled with the thermostat.

"Thanks again for letting me hang out here. My hotel won't have power until tomorrow, at the earliest."

"You get what you pay for," Nikki said, trying to start some banter.

She was right about that. Matt must do well for himself since they were staying at a place that per night easily rivaled my entire vacation cost. It did lack the homey and unique vibe that was provided at The Desert Inn. This was the kind of place boring people stayed at. The type of people who can throw money at problems and make them go away. The sort of person who just has someone else book their vacations for them. The ones who haven't even been to a Priceline or Orbitz and created their own itinerary. The most exciting thing that could have happened here was a prom date losing her virginity, or a highly esteemed businessman meeting his mistress when he said he was going on a business trip. I guarantee someone has been murdered in my hotel. It's nothing to brag about, it's just some sort of character.

Nikki took a couple of personally sized white wine bottles from the mini-bar, pulled the wine glasses from the rack above the sink to pour us each a drink. She had changed over the last few days. The girl I talked to at the slushie bar that initially just thought her husband was going to be a little distant and play some golf was growing more panicked. The hope in this being just a disastrous vacation was dying. I could see that she believed this was going to be the rest of her life; that if she were going to stay with Matt, she would always be a second, or third, or fifth priority. This was accentuated when she came over and handed me the wine, and I noticed she was slightly trembling, and there were dark bags under her eyes.

"Where's Matt?" I asked as I took a sip.

"I'm not sure."

"Is he going to be mad when there's a strange man in his room?"

"He's not coming back here."

She downed the drink entirely and exhaled, embracing the burn of cheap wine. She reached into her purse next to the bed and rooted around for several moments until she pulled out her Newports. She took one out of the pack along with a lighter and started smoking in the hotel room.

"He went back to Texas," she said after she took a drag.

"Why?"

"Business," she said coldly. Nikki then started waving her arms around trying to get the smoke away from her, but the air was stagnant, and the smoke was lingering around us. She promptly got up and opened the window and balcony door.

"Holy shit!" I blurted out, "Yours open?"

"What do you mean?"

"They told me at my hotel we couldn't open our windows or balconies because of turtles or something."

"What the hell are you talking about?" Nikki asked cocking her head to the side and blowing smoke out of the corner of her mouth.

"Nevermind."

Nikki's attention turned to her cigarette. She watched the smoke slowly dance off the end of it and then quickly vanish out of the open window. After a while, she went over and opened another personally sized bottle of wine and made herself another glass. She didn't take this one like a shot though. She slowly sipped it, and her attention dashed from her cigarette, then to her drink, and then back to me.

"Do you remember the other day when you were saying it wasn't one thing that led to your divorce, it was a bunch of little things?"

I nodded.

"I know what you mean now. I understood it before on a simpler level, but I really get it now."

"You don't know that."

Nikki rolled her eyes, and she took another large sip of wine, almost finishing off her glass again.

"This is just a honeymoon. Don't take it so seriously."

"It's not just the honeymoon. I have been thinking about how this was a mistake for a while. Even before the marriage."

Nikki walked toward me and sat down on the bed next to me. She gently put her hand on my leg and looked at me, and it felt like she looked right through me. Her eyes began to well up with tears, and they started silently falling into her lap. I looked down not knowing how to help her and watched the hot, salty tears splatter dots onto her jeans. She gently moved her hand from my leg and onto my face, forcing me to look back at her.

"You're the only person who has really talked to me about this." Her voice quivering as she spoke.

"There is no way that's true Nik-."

"It is true," she snapped back. "My husband, my friends, my parents, I was forced into this. These decisions were just made for me, and I didn't do what I wanted to do."

"A part of you has to-"

"Stop standing up for him!" She yelled, knowing what I was going to say, "You don't even know him."

"I hardly know you!"

This statement upset Nikki, and she lowered her head. Her body started convulsing, and tears began streaming down her face. I didn't know what to do. When Linda and I were together, supporting her emotionally was something I struggled with. Truthfully, any situation that requires intense and immediate consoling is something I have never been able to do quite right. People are usually offended when I say cliché statements like, 'Everything will be fine,' or, 'These things happen for a reason.' People also don't appreciate a friendly pat on the back or shoulder.

"I should go," I said. I abruptly stood up to leave, but she grabbed my wrist and looked up at me, tears still rolling down her face that was becoming red and puffy. I sat back down and said, "You're lucky you're a really, really ugly crier."

We both uncomfortably laughed, and Nikki immediately said in almost a whisper, "Please, don't leave."

"I don't think that's a good idea, Nikki."

"I don't care. I don't care what everyone else thinks is right, I just want to do what I think is right."

The room was quiet for a minute until she stood up, without saying a word, and made her way toward the bathroom. She stopped in the doorway and turned around and looked back, and for a minute she stared at me, quiet and contemplative, but her face slowly softened. She smiled and moved her hand to the light switch and turned it off, and just for the briefest of moments we were lost with each other with only the sounds of the waves crashing and the seagulls cawing into the deep, deep twilight. In the dark, we forgot it all.

14

I woke up to the sound of the phone ringing next to the bed. Without opening my eyes, I grabbed it, and nearly yelled into the receiver, "I said no calls." I slammed it down and tried to roll over to get back to sleep.

Then the phone rang again. Although it was impossible I would have sworn it was somehow ringing louder than before. I picked it up ready to yell into the receiver, but before I could a polite young woman meekly said, "I'm sorry sir, I do know you said you wanted your calls held, but checkout is in one hour, and your wife just left the hotel, checking you two out a few days early."

My eyes shot open and I realized I wasn't at The Desert Inn. I was in way too nice of a hotel. "My wife?" I finally asked perplexed.

"Yes, sir," she said after a few seconds of silence. "You're on your honeymoon, right?"

"Of course," I responded only half listening to the question. I was busy scanning the room. "Thank you." I hung up the phone still trying to wake up from one of the more unusual nights I've had since being separated. The room was empty. No sign of Nikki, just like the receptionist said. There were just a few empty bottles strewn across the hotel room and cigarette butts extinguished in a half drank wine glasses.

I thought Nikki would be ok, but now I was having issues understanding what just happened. I wasn't sure if she slept with me to get revenge on her husband, or because she wanted to feel better about herself, to have a reason to get a divorce, or just because she felt sorry for me. Whatever the reason she didn't want to stick around to explain it.

I grabbed my board shorts and shirt I had worn the night before and made sure I had my phone and wallet. It took less than a minute to get everything, and I made my way out into the hallway. While the door closed behind me I looked back into the hotel room and saw the wind blowing the curtains, wisping them up and pushing them into the wine glass. I saw the half empty glass filled with half smoked cigarettes fall to the ground and as the door shut, I heard it pop onto the ground and shatter. Then it was quiet again. I realized with no Nikki in Florida I really didn't have much of a reason to stick around for a few more days. Also, my bank account couldn't support the reckless drinking I had been doing. Despite the fact that I had nothing to go back to, that's when I knew it was time to leave Florida.

WELCOME HOME

1

"You look hungover," Mom said. Her arms were crossed, and she was glaring at me. The television boomed in the background as a crowd erupted, elated about something. Dad turned his head from the game and looked at me, just for a moment, then looked back at the TV.

"I am hungover," I said.

"How was Florida?" She asked, disinterested.

"Good."

"Why didn't you talk to Linda?"

Just then Jackson came around the corner. His pupils dilated, and he let out a short, soft meow before walking up to me and rubbing on my legs. I picked him up, and as I cradled him, he purred so quietly it was almost inaudible.

"He hasn't been interested in us at all," Mom said sternly. "He didn't even let us touch him. He just runs away and eats when we're all out of the house or asleep."

"Yeah, he can be skittish sometimes. Especially with new people."

"Steve," Mom tried to get us back on track, "I set up a meeting with you and Linda. She needs you right now."

"Mom, I-"

"Steven," she interrupted, "I know you're upset about the way she separated from you. I know you're flying high on this independence streak you've got going, and I know you feel like you have Linda reeling, just like she had you reeling. Please, I beg of you, look past your pride and forgive your wife. You can have your entire life back. You can get your job back. You can be safe again."

"Mom, please."

"Listen to your mother, Steve," Dad said in a deep tone, without turning his head toward me.

"I just feel like the last few months you have been adrift. Confused. Unable to get out of this funk. Nobody can snap you out of it except you because nobody owes you anything."

"I just-"

"I don't care what you think you need, Steven." Her voice was getting louder. Jackson buried his face into my arm and hid his eyes from Mom, "You two are meeting at The Lowry, and that's final. This is non-negotiable."

"Mom, why are you trying so hard to save a marriage neither of us wants?"

"She wants it, Steve."

"Well, she should have thought about that before asking for a separation."

"You've got to let that go, son," Dad interjected eyes transfixed on the television.

"Why though?" I asked.

"To make everything go back to normal," Mom said.

She believed it too. She really did. I could see it in her eyes. She and Dad had so many arguments, broken up and got back together so many times that this was run of the mill. My situation was just like any other fight for them.

"Mom, I don't want things to go back. Even if I wanted to, I can't go back."

"You're new to marriage. I am telling you, this is the way it is sometimes."

"Can you just make a goddamned basket?" My Dad yelled in the background.

"Mom, this whole thing just feels-"

"Hard?" She interjected.

"No."

"Impossible?"

"No, Mom. It feels, empty."

She looked at me, genuinely befuddled. She then stared at Jackson who was starting to squirm in my arms.

"It's not too late to go back. I know it, Steven."

"Even if that were true, after all of this, why would I even want to go back?"

"Because that's what you do when you're married to someone. You stick together. You promised no matter what happened you would grow together and be there through thick and thin. That even when you didn't want to, you would put each other first."

"Well, then I probably made a huge mistake."

Mom's mouth was agape. The rage and anger that she had met me with initially, turned to sadness and frustration. This was something that she could never understand because no matter what happened between her and Dad, she would always find a way to make the marriage work.

"You do what you want, Steven. Just don't expect us to support you or your decisions."

The crowd once again screamed, and my Dad stood up and yelled at the television. I couldn't tell if it was out of happiness or anger. Mom's frustration turned to him for a moment, but he didn't notice.

"I set up a meeting for you two at The Lowry for tomorrow morning," she said, trying to portray a neutral, emotionless tone. "Even if this is your choice, please, just do this one thing for me."

"Do I even have a choice?" I asked.

It went unanswered.

2

"How was your trip?" Linda asked before I sat down.

"Fine," I replied.

"What did you do?"

"Not very much."

"Then why couldn't you call me back?" Linda looked concerned. "I talked with your Mom. She said she talked to you about everything and thought we could figure things out."

"Welcome to The Lowry, you two," a friendly voice exclaimed from the side of the table. "What would you like to drink?"

"What's your favorite beer?" I asked the waitress.

"That would be Todd Axe Man," she replied, "I had a keg of it at my wedding. It's very popular."

"I'll have one of those," I replied.

"Steven," Linda said, looking concerned across the table, "it's 11:30 in the morning."

"In that case, I'll have a Bloody Mary, with Todd the Axe Man as a chaser."

The waitress giggled. Linda continued to glare at me, slowly turning her look to the waitress.

"Anything for you?" She asked smiling at Linda.

"I'll just have water."

The waitress jotted it down in her notepad, smiled again at us, and went off to the bar.

"She must be new."

"What makes you say that?" Linda asked.

"I just don't remember her from after our sessions. That and she's writing everything down."

Linda fidgeted. I could tell there was discomfort and panic in her eyes because she didn't ever think she would be the one with her back against the ropes. This was getting very embarrassing for her. This wasn't a trendy 'I'm going to leave my husband' scenario anymore. She wasn't showcasing her power over me, and I wasn't a broken man who was desperately fighting for her back. Leaving me was a gamble, and at this point, it was clear she had bet on the wrong horse.

"I talked to father today," she said abruptly.

"Ok."

"He said you can have your job back, but it will have to be back at entry level."

"Tell him no."

"Listen, it would just be for a little bit, then-"

"I'm not saying 'no' to the entry level, I'm saying 'no' to the entire thing."

"Then where are you going to work?"

"I'm not sure."

"Well, I would hurry up because the bank account is dwindling."

"Then maybe you should stop taking money out of it."

"I just took money out because we still agreed to split bills while we were separated. I'm not ripping you off, Steve," she said sympathetically. "Even if we're taking a break, or going through a divorce, or whatever, I need to know what are you going to do for work."

Our waitress came over and put down my Bloody Mary and Linda's water. She was turning to walk away, and I blurted out, "Hey, are you guys hiring?"

She looked at me, puzzled. "I don't think so," was all she said, and she hastily walked away from our table.

"Worth a shot." I picked up my Bloody Mary and took a spicy sip.

"Any other ideas?" Linda sneered.

"That was pretty much it for now."

Linda's face was stoic and calm for most of the meeting, but it was beginning to contort into the angry face I had seen so many times. White, hot rage bubbled underneath her thin skin, and I thought she was going to lose control. Then she stopped. She inhaled, then exhaled slowly, shutting her eyes and trying to ignore how frustrating this meeting was.

"You haven't asked about Jackson," I said as I took out the pickle in the Blood Mary.

"Steve," Linda said exhausted, "I need a favor."

"What kind of favor?"

"A big one."

I took another gulp of the Bloody Mary, and looked at Linda. Her eyes were welling up with tears.

"Father is sick, Steve," she said coldly.

"Ok."

"We don't know the details yet. Whether that is because of father not wanting to tell us the information, or the doctor not knowing, I am not sure. All we know is it is an advanced form of cancer."

"That sucks."

"One thing I know is that doctors recommend a low-stress environment for cancer patients. The more stress, the more likely it is that the patient-"

"Can you please just tell me what you want?"

"Just for a while can we please keep up the idea that we're going to stay married?"

"What?"

"Just hear me out," Linda said in a panic filled, trembling voice. "I know things aren't good between us, and I know that you aren't interested in being with me anymore. I understand all of that. Can you please, just do this for me?"

I didn't respond. This is the kind of stuff that men who get dumped or divorced dream of. One day she says she's leaving you, and the next here she is, hat in hand, begging for you to come back. Not only because she wants to try and figure things out, but because she needs you to come back so her dad can live.

"I don't want to answer this right now," I started. "This whole situation is pretty messy, and I don't want to make a promise that I'll feel uncomfortable keeping later."

"Steven. Please." Tears started to cascade down her face. "The only reason I need to know now is because you have dodged my calls for weeks."

"Can you just give me a real reason I should even consider this?"

"Because even if we're not married now, we were still married once. If there were anyone else who could do this, I would ask them. Please."

"I'll go once."

"Once what? A month?"

"No, just one time."

"Steven."

"No. Once. That's my final offer. I'm conceding to you by going. You have to give me something here."

"That won't convince him."

"Then lie more convincingly."

Linda breathed deeply again, trying to get control of herself. She wasn't used to this. In the past, she called the shots. She would be the one to say when, where, and how much. That overarching power was gone, and she was left with an unrelenting, hard 'no' that she didn't know how to overcome. When she didn't get into the University of Minnesota because her grades were hardly good enough to graduate high school, her dad made calls and ensured sure she could still go. When she needed me to go to a party, I had to wear a particular outfit, clear my schedule, and tell certain jokes. When Linda wanted us to make more money, she sold my soul to the company her father worked for. Up until now, it was all on her terms. Everything was confined to what she needed. But if she was comfortably watching the world through a glass bubble, I was a crack that had popped into existence. I was rooting and branching further and deeper and soon it would shatter.

The panic was flooding to her face, and I saw hives breaking out on her shoulders.

"Let me know where I should meet you two," I said as I got up and started to leave the restaurant. She didn't say anything as I did. I felt confident and content, but the frigid air snapped me back into reality as I walked out into the unforgiving winter.

I realized that up until this point I was the victim of the situation. Linda left me, she moved out, she pushed me away. Everything could be easily explained as Linda being the bad guy. Although I didn't care about her gossipy friends before or after our separation, it wasn't hard to figure out that this decision looked terrible on her part. Most of her friends and family didn't love me, but they didn't hate me either. They all looked at me like they would a floral wallpaper at a nursing home or an IKEA coffee table. I was just there. No frills. Nothing special. Only there for some inane reason. She wasn't running away from an abusive husband or a bum who didn't contribute to the household. Her friends' initial murmurs of confusion, transformed into rumors of a scandal. Her Facebook posts had changed from, "And still, she persisted," and thoughts of independence to lonely ones about watching *Friends* and complaining about living with her parents.

I only speculated this because of the way she was laying it on in The Lowry. This was a strategic move. This was her way of showing that I was, indeed, a terrible husband. What kind of a person wouldn't go visit their spouse's sick father more than once? A neglectful one. That was how this could be presented. I, Steve Harding, am a terrible, terrible person.

The wind whipped again, and my ears and nose went numb. I missed Florida. I couldn't tell you why, but I did. Maybe more than missing Florida, I just hated leaving it for Minnesota. I pulled out my phone and fiddled through it until I saw Nikki's name. I had a picture in her contact information, and it was from a day we spent walking on the boardwalk together. She was wearing a baby blue bathing suit, and her hair was blowing straight up as she was closing one eye to prevent it from being whipped by the wind. I couldn't remember actually taking the picture, and I couldn't even tell you what day I did. We were both so drunk so often that my memory of the trip is pretty much just a blur of being by the beach and drinking. We were just continuously laughing, and talking, and smoking cigarettes. Not one day stands out because they were all the same. They were all so good. They were all forgettable.

I hung my finger over the, "Call," button, but I couldn't bring myself to do it. I wanted to know how she was doing and why she left without saying goodbye. I wanted to know if her situation had improved and if I would ever see her again. But I couldn't. The memory of waking up alone in that hotel room shook me deep and back into reality. I felt humiliated and confused, and I didn't want to talk to a person who left me with no explanation.

I flipped through my other contacts and got to John. "Want a drink?" I texted him. Without waiting for a response, I went to the bus stop and waited for the next ride to take me downtown.

"It's not even noon," he replied, but he didn't say no.

Troy Bernardo

3

"You don't look any more tan," John said through a wide grin. He tossed his laptop bag into the booth and sat down in front of the beer I had ordered him.

"I didn't spend a lot of time sunbathing at the beach."

"Weren't you staying at the beach?"

"Yeah, I mean, I went to the beach and spent time outside, but I never actually went to the beach just to get sun."

"You are just a waste of a life. You know that?"

"People who go to the beach to get darker when they can just lay around in the air conditioning are the wastes of life."

"So, what did you do for the whole vacation?"

"I just relaxed. I drank, walked around, went to the boardwalk, made some friends."

"You think you'll stay in touch with any of them?"

"Probably not."

John glared at me. Not because he was mad, but because he knew I wasn't telling the whole truth.

"How's everything going with you?" I asked, changing the subject.

"Not the best." He said with a suspicious tone. "Sarah and I have a flea infestation."

"How did that happen?"

"Who cares?" He said, "What is going on with you lately, man? Are you coming back to work?"

"Jesus, you sound like Linda."

"You met with Linda and didn't tell me?"

"It happened today."

"When?"

"This morning."

"What did you talk about?"

"Her Dad is dying and-"

"My boss', boss', boss is dying?"

"Yeah, by the way, don't tell anyone that. Anyways, she wants me to spend time with her and her Dad to make him less stressed."

"So? You're going to do it?"

"I told her I'd give her a day."

John's face turned a dark, deep red and he was clenching his beer so hard I thought the glass would shatter.

"Well, I think that's a real dick thing to do, Steve," he said in a serious tone.

"Well, if that's the case maybe you shouldn't think about it."

John slammed his beer down on the table with a loud *thud* spilling a good amount, and most the bar turned to look at us.

"What do you want, Steve? Do you want people to feel sorry for you? Do you want independence? Is this all just some elaborate way of being an asshole to everyone who is trying to help you? Grow up. Nobody cares about the problems you created or your self-loathing bullshit."

I stood up and put a ten-dollar bill on the table. I looked down at John. He was cartoonishly red, and I could tell that if I was there any longer, it was going to result in a fight. "Thanks for the pep talk, John," I said. "Also, you can cover the rest of the tab for being such a dick."

"Fuck you, Steve!" He yelled.

I walked out of the bar and toward my bus stop.

4

"Can you tell me why you think you'd be a good fit for the Super America family?" Bill said, not lifting his eyes from my resume and application. He dressed like a corporate man through and through. The black tie seemed a bit formal for a gas station manager, but his stained white shirt contrasted it. Not vague stains though. Food stains. I saw two dime-sized mustard blotches on his tie and a red ketchup stain on his elbow. His nametag read:

Super America
Bill M.
Manager

"I just need a job right now," I replied.
"Why?" He asked.
"Because I need money."
"What for?"
"Living?" I responded.
I don't think he appreciated the answer, and he noted something on my resume.
"I'm going to level with you, Bill. My wife left me a few months ago. I worked for her dad and I had to quit because I hated the job and it had become tense around the office. I just need money. I need this job."
Bill's face lifted from my resume. He raised an eyebrow and stared at me, sizing me up. Even if he was confused by the interaction and my bluntness, he was tired of filling this role over and over again with seventeen-year-olds who didn't show up for work.
"If we do hire you, what can you bring to the table? Why should we let you work here?"
"I'm professional, I don't call in sick, and I will be on time. I know other people who apply for this job say that, but I mean it. I need this job. Not like a college kid who needs this so he can save up some money for Bonnaroo tickets. I need it to live."
This wasn't the interview Bill was used to. He put down the resume and leaned back in his chair. He licked his lips and took off his glasses, massaging the space between the corners of his eyes. After a few moments he looked at me and said, "Listen, I understand you're going through a rough time. I know this job isn't going to fulfill you or give you any more than just a paycheck. This resume is impressive; impressive enough to hire you directly as a manager here. You have more corporate experience than I have and truthfully, you just seem overqualified for the positions we have open."

"I'm not applying to be a manager," I replied.

"You do understand that if you got this job, you wouldn't have a team under you. You would be mopping the floors, putting money on pumps, selling cigarettes and lottery tickets, and even cleaning the hot dog grill. Is that something you're prepared to do? Because if I'm being honest, you could probably take this resume to any downtown temp agency and they could get you clerical work, for much more money, by the end of the week."

"Why are you trying to talk me out of working for you?"

"I don't want to spend the time and resources training you to realize in a week that this isn't a good fit. I know that selling condoms and slushies to sixteen-year-olds might be your calling, but doing it for $8.50 an hour might get old too."

"I'm sure all of these things will get old, Bill. I'm sure after my second or third overnight I won't like the job, and returning to corporate America will be appealing. I'd be lying if I told you I actually want this job. That being said, there isn't anywhere else at this point I want to work at. I won't be quitting in a month and I won't be submitting my resume to a temp agency, not because I undervalue my time and experiences there, but because returning would be worse than selling condoms and cigarettes."

Bill closed his eyes again and let out a long, low exhale. After a few moments, I said, "Worst case scenario is you're right, and I don't hack it here. If I'm right though, you have smart, experienced, reliable employee who won't bail on his shifts. Really, the risk of hiring me is no greater than hiring another 16-year-old because of the turn over anyways."

Bill laughed heartily. He then weighed his options, genuinely considering what would be in his best interest. I did make a good point. What did he have to lose? He stood up and extended his hand, saying, "I hope you're right. You can start tomorrow if you want."

We shook on it.

"I won't let you down, Bill."

"Either way it's fine."

5

"I remember when I was a kid and they used to ask me what I wanted to be when I grew up, but I never had an answer. Even when my teachers would tell me to suspend all my ideas of what I should do, or what I was good at; I still couldn't come up with anything to say. I don't think anyone really knew though. Anyone who had an answer just went off of what their parents had told them." I threw the empty can into the pile and opened another of my 24-ounce cans of Miller Lite. The fizz sprayed on my lap. It was warm, and the taste was initially repulsive.

"Those kids who said they wanted to be doctors and lawyers just said that because that's what their dads did. This one kid in my class, KC, said he wanted to be a cop just like his father, and I think he's been arrested a half a dozen times. Nothing big. Small time shit like marijuana possession, driving with a suspended license, petty theft, but still an impressive tear. The kids who said they wanted to be artists just said that because their parents wanted them to be. None of them, or their parents, really wanted that though. I bet today, almost all of them are salesmen, or account managers, working some other dead-end job."

I took another sip to moisten my mouth. It was becoming dry because of all the talking.

"I don't know one outstanding person from my graduating class. Not an author. Not a musician. Not an athlete. Nothing. Most of them just had some banal dream that never materialized, because when you turn eighteen everyone tells you to stop talking and sit down in class. Everyone loses their individuality while they're trying to carve it out. Everyone thinks they're special in a world filled with people exactly like them. Me, though? I just never had an answer. Even if the other kids had dreams that weren't theirs at least they had something. The only thing I left school with was admission to a new school, and then Linda, and then a job working for her dad. People keep talking to me like I need to wake up, but why? My life isn't over. Even with a job at a gas station, a married woman who won't talk to me, my marriage clearly damaged beyond repair, and losing one of my only friends, it feels more real and meaningful than it ever has."

I took another gulp of the warm, foamy beer and nearly gagged.

"This is the perfect example, buddy." I said after my body stopped rejecting the alcohol. "This is the perfect way to celebrate getting a new job. You and me just hanging out, drinking, and letting it all hang out."

Jackson looked at me again. Even though he was just a cat, he looked concerned. When I would put the beer back on the coffee table he would relax, but the sound of the crinkling can would awaken his anxiety again and he would let out soft meows during my soliloquies. He would also get alarmed when I would open a new beer. The sound would make him alert and he would stand up and circle his pillow again before falling back in a shallow sleep.

"Jackson, I'm not sure if it's sad or enlightening that you're now my best friend."

He perked himself up, and then his eyes dilated and danced around the room. Then he kneaded into the pillow on the ground trying to get comfortable once again. Before Linda got him, he was a feral kitten. The biggest house and the best cat food could never take that out of him. But his skittish, cold nature was reserved for everyone else except me. Maybe he saw something in me. Maybe he believed in me. Maybe he had a sixth sense and could see down into the person I truly am. Or maybe I was just drunk, and he was a cat.

BAM BAM BAM

Jackson jolted up as our conversation was interrupted by three sudden, staccato slams at the door. I immediately knew this was not going to be fun, and I tried to sober up before I answered. It had been a busy and confrontational day to say the least. It was easy to think that this could be nearly anyone who I talked with in the last twelve hours. A disgruntled wife, an angry family member, a frustrated in-law, John, all of these were terrifying, realistic possibilities. Worried picking up the mess of the living room would be too loud and give away my binge drinking, I threw a blanket over the pile of beer cans in the corner of the room and made my way to the door. I opened it to see Paul, the landlord, staring at me with the fake smile he always had. It's difficult to say what exactly made his smile so questionable. It reminded me of John Elway's smile. Maybe some of his teeth weren't real. Perhaps he had a face that I didn't trust, or he was just insincere. Whatever the reason, Paul tended to put me on edge.

"Hey, Paul," I said a clearly as I could. "What can I do for you?"

"Hey, Steve," He said through his grin. "I'm sorry to stop by so late, I just wanted to talk to you about the rent."

"Sure, Paul," I responded. I tried to say as little as possible to mask how drunk I was.

"Well, I know you've been going through a rough time, and I have been pretty liberal with the rent due dates and whatnot. When my first wife left me, it really messed me up for a while, and I wanted to make sure you were ok too."

"Thanks," I replied.

"The reason I'm here is because, well, the last check you sent me bounced."

"Shit."

"It's ok, I'm not going to evict you or even get mad about this. Your wife probably has access to your bank account still and has been withdrawing money."

"How did you know that?"

Paul looked at me with a surprised stare that went on for an uncomfortably long period of time. Then he let out a hearty laugh that resonated through the dark, empty streets.

"Steve," he started with that smile still strung across his face, "you're a good kid, and I want you to know that before I say this. Absolutely nothing you're going through is new. Shit, when I went through my first divorce, my ex-wife burned all my clothes in the front yard. This situation isn't even remotely unique. I know it feels that way. I know everything feels like it's falling apart, and to some extent it is, but this happens every day to people. Actually, I bet it happens every hour, if not every minute. Half of all marriages end like this, man. Try not to take it personally."

"I don't think that's very fair, Paul. You don't know what is going on between Linda and me."

"That's true. I don't know exactly what your situation is," he said nodding his head sincerely, "But I bet I have a pretty good idea."

We stood there for a minute because neither of us knew what to say. We looked at each other as a few cars drove by on the street behind him and he continued to smile.

"I'll talk to Linda and figure out the money. We'll move some stuff around." I said, defeated.

"Good. Can you try to get it figured out by this weekend?"

"Yeah. I'll straighten it out tonight."

"Don't push it bud, and if you need more time or help, just let me know."

"Thanks, Paul. I will."

Paul nodded and wandered off into the cold Minneapolis night, after about ten steps, he turned around and jovially exclaimed, "Welcome to the divorced club, Steve." He laughed to himself in the empty streets as I closed the door and he went off into the snowdrifts and ice.

6

"For today, I just want you behind the counter. Don't worry about anything else. Don't clean the bathrooms, don't put new hotdogs on, don't clean up any aisles. Just punch in the numbers when people want gas and sell people cigarettes and beer."

The fluorescent lights felt like they were burning holes through my eyes, deep into my brain. I could feel the searing pain of stomach acid halfway up my throat. I was so groggy and confused that walking the four blocks to work was bewildering and exhausting.

Despite the late hour, I was obscenely hungover.

"Is there a reason I'm not doing any of these things?" I asked before taking a sip of my coffee.

"Listen, Steve, do you want this job? Because if you do, we need to ease you in. If you see the atrocities that go on in a bathroom here on a daily basis, you will quit by the end of the day. I once found a dead junkie out behind the dumpster. My first week, a guy bought honey, whipped cream, and condoms and asked for the bathroom key. Since I was new, I gave it to him. Later that night the bathroom was a disgusting mess of...well...you get it." Bill only stopped because a few young teenagers walked into the empty store. He nodded at me and started to make his way back to the back office.

"I remember why I wanted this job." I said sarcastically.

"So you could show up hungover?"

"At least I showed up. Weren't there supposed to be two of us here for training?"

"Actually, three. Two of them are a lot smarter than you," he said, without even turning back as he faded into his office. "Oh, one more thing," he said nonchalantly, "if someone tried to rob the place, just give them what they want. We have insurance for shit like that. Don't be a hero."

I turned to the teenagers who were gathering Hot Cheetos and coffee for their evening snack. One of them looked around and put a pack of gum in his back pocket. I was too hungover and new to care.

7

At the end of my first shift, the sun wasn't even close to rising. I had worked from 8:00 p.m. to 4:00 a.m. When I asked Bill why he gave out such an awful shift to a new employee, he said something along the lines of, "It thins out the crowd." I wandered down the empty streets and started doing the math in my head for how much I earned for the night. I figured at close to eight dollars an hour for eight hours, I made $64. Pre-tax of course. I had to work 160 hours, and I would almost be able to make rent without asking Linda for help or Paul for another extension.

Despite the adversity, I knew I could do it. Maybe I'd pick up an extra job as a pizza delivery guy, or I could tutor like I used to do in college. I'd have to brush up on some courses, but it was a possibility. I could even sell some of my old records and books. It was time to get industrious and work on getting my life together. It was time for me to start over if that's what I really wanted. It was time for action. Under the lights that illuminated the streets, I saw quick flashes of glittering, aimless snow drifts. I was distracted, but routine and instinct guided me the few blocks back to my front door, and in the clear, freezing morning air I felt peaceful and calm. My hangover was gone, and I was engulfed in exhaustion.

I took out my keys, and unlocked my door. It felt good to be home. It felt good to really have a vision for what my next steps were going to be. Most of all, it felt good to have something that was truly mine. Even if in a few months Linda wanted to take the apartment back, for now, it was mine, and nobody could take that away from me. Not her dad being my boss, not my parents disapproving of the divorce, not John, and definitely not Linda.

As I opened the door. The serene calmness from outside continued. There was no sound or scurrying from Jackson on the floor as he usually did whenever I got home.

That's when I saw Jackson on the floor right next to my couch. He was twitching, and foam was coming out of his mouth. Every few seconds, his body would constrict, and then he would extend his head and extremities in unnatural and terrifying ways. For what could have only been a few seconds, I stood there, watching Jackson flail uncontrollably on the ground. I grabbed the blanket off my hidden beer cans and scooped him into my arms. He continued to convulse unnaturally, but I had to do something. I just tried to cradle him as he moved and seized randomly, and went out to my car.

8

I burst into the veterinary hospital with Jackson in my arms. His erratic movements had stopped, and he just was looking around. He seemed disoriented and confused, but not alarmed by the other animals in the vet's waiting room. I could tell he wasn't scared because his eyes turned black, and dilated to unreal proportions when he is afraid.

"Can somebody help?" I said panicked and frustrated.

An older woman quickly came out from the back of a desk, wearing scrubs and had a stethoscope wrapped around her neck. She walked briskly over to me and looked at Jackson bundled up in the blanket.

"Are you the one who just called?" She asked in a quiet, soothing voice.

"Yes."

"You think he's having some sort of seizure?" She asked.

I nodded in agreement.

"This is Jackson then?"

I nodded again.

She grabbed the blanket and moved it so she could see Jackson's face. His eyes were closed and he was softly purring. She smiled and said, "Don't worry. This is normal. This is what we call the 'post-ictal' phase. Has he ever had a seizure before?"

"No." I replied.

"How long did the seizure last?"

"I don't know. I was at work when it started."

"Well, once you got home, how long did it last?"

"Five minutes? Maybe seven?"

She put the ear tips of the stethoscope in her ears and put the diaphragm on Jackson's chest. After a few seconds she said, "Generally, for us to seek treatment, we need to know the severity of the seizures and frequency of them," she said calmly. "What I recommend is letting us run a few tests and potentially putting Jackson on some medicine. I need to be upfront though, because of the duration of seizure there's a good chance I will recommend putting him on Phenobarbital." She motioned to hold Jackson, and I handed the stale, beer soaked blanket to her.

"Whatever will make him better," I said.

"We have a lot of success with this medicine. I think he will be fine as long as he stays on it."

Relief washed over me as I covered Jackson back up because he was trying to obstruct the lights with his paw. I felt guilty that I was at work when this all started and felt embarrassed that I wasn't there for him when he needed me the most. All this for $64.

"How much do you think all of this will cost?" I asked.

The older woman's face got more serious. She looked at me, a little scared. She already knew I wasn't going to like the answer. Unfortunately, in her line of work, that often meant the pet wasn't going to get the treatment and was going to be put down.

"It's going to be relatively expensive."

"How expensive is 'relatively' expensive?"

"The tests will be somewhere around $400 to $500. Then the medicine will probably be close to $6 a day."

"That's...that's over $2000 a year," I said. "Not even including the tests you're doing today."

"I know it's a lot to ask," she said in that mild, quiet whisper. "I often have to give bad news to nice pet owners like yourself. The best you can make this decision is asking yourself if Jackson would do it for you."

Hot tears ran down my cheeks, and I broke out into a smile, saying, "I think he's the only one who would do it for me." The woman looked at me, as she cradled Jackson in her arms, transfixed that I had said something both so heartwarming and incredibly depressing. Yet our shared moment was a complex regularity in her day to day dealings with both animals and their owners.

"Do whatever you need to do. How long will the tests take?"

"A few hours at least. Then after that, we would like to keep him for examination for a few hours." She carefully handed Jackson to her assistant as she grabbed a clipboard off the front desk. "If you fill out these forms with your cell phone number, we can contact you when they're finished."

I watched the assistant carry Jackson into the back room, and I took the clipboard and forms from her and calmly replied, "I'd rather just wait."

I sat down in one of the available seats and settled in for a long morning. As I was filling out the paperwork, I thought about Jackson and how far we both had come since Linda brought him home. I remembered discovering fleas and ringworm on him the first week we had adopted him because he was missing fur on his paw and how he was continually itching himself. I thought back to cleaning up his throw-up because he wasn't used to his new food, and how I was the one who was always changing out his water bowl and sifting through his litter box. Sure, the relationship seemed one-sided on paper, but it made more sense than any of the other ones I had.

9

"Hey, wake up, dude." A young teenage boy was poking me with a broomstick. He was wearing scrubs for some reason even though it seemed like he was just cleaning the floors.

"Why the fuck are you waking me up?"

"They're done with your cat. He's down the hall in room three."

I got up and checked my pockets to make sure I hadn't dropped anything while I had been asleep. It had been a long morning, and the sun was high in the sky. I looked at my phone and saw several missed calls and realized it was already 2:45. That meant I had been here for well over eight hours; a good portion of which I had been asleep.

When I got to door three I realized it was slightly ajar. I knocked quietly, and I could see through the sliver that the same woman who took Jackson earlier was standing behind a metal desk, petting him softly on his back. She noticed that I could see her and gently gestured for me to come in. Jackson started to get up but was too tired to actually get all the way into a sitting position. Instead, he meowed hoarsely and nestled back down into his arms. The woman smiled at me.

"Jackson did very well on his tests," she said calmly. "So, we think he is ready to go home."

"What about the medication?" I asked.

"We will get you his prescription on the way out."

Jackson tried to meow again, but only mimed the action.

"Why isn't he up? Why is he so tired?"

"That's often just a result of the seizure. I wouldn't worry too much about it. He should be back to his normal self in just a few days." She grabbed the blanket I had brought Jackson in, handed it to me, and smiled. "You're a good owner," she said softly.

"Thanks."

"I mean it!" She fired back, showing the first true emotions I had seen from her, "Do you know how many scumbag people I deal with? I've seen owners put down their pets over much less than this. I'm glad you are taking this responsibility seriously. If we had more people like you, we wouldn't have to kill so many helpless pets."

"Thank you," I said more sincerely.

She nodded at me and left the room, and I wrapped Jackson in the blanket and started to make my way out of the office. I could hear his soft purrs as we walked and he looked at me exhausted, but somehow lucid. I could have sworn he had a subtle smile.

10

We got back home, and I lowered Jackson onto the couch. He was in a deep sleep now and was still getting over the trauma of the day. I reached in my pocket and pulled out a receipt from the vet. The charge for the medicine, the stay, and the tests totaled $773.98, and I knew that a new prescription was going to be needed in a month and a half for another $300. I pinned the receipt on the corkboard next to the front door and stared at it. I was going to need money. A lot of money. Very fast.

I took out my phone and called Bill. It rang a few times and then I heard, "Steve?"

"Hey, Bill."

"Let me guess, you're not coming to work today."

"Yeah, I'm sorry."

"Are you quitting?"

"No! I love the job."

"Then what's up?"

"My cat had a seizure last night."

"Your cat? How did you get a cat?" I thought this was an odd question. 'How did you get a cat?' Who asks something like that?

"The pound?"

"It's ok Steve., thanks for the call. You think you'll be in tomorrow?"

"As long as Jackson doesn't have another seizure, I'll be there."

"Good," Bill said, and then he hung up. I put the phone in my pocket and took a second to consider what I had to do next.

Silence cloaked the apartment in a false sense of peace. I turned away from the corkboard and made my way to the couch to sit next to Jackson. Usually, when I sat down next to him, he would walk to my lap and sit for warmth and attention. He didn't do that though. He was just lying there fast asleep. I picked him up and placed him on my lap and stroked the top of his head gently. He didn't purr, but he did involuntarily knead the air.

I took my phone back out and scrolled through my contacts. I was looking for someone, anyone who could help me with this situation. The longer I scrolled, the more I realized what I already knew. There was only one person who would help me.

I punched Linda's number in and waited for a few rings. "Hello?" Linda answer groggily.

"It's like three in the afternoon," I said.

"I know."

"I need your help."

"Why would I help you?"

"Fair question. This isn't entirely for me though."

Silence.

"Linda, can you just come over to the apartment? We have some important matters we need to discuss."

"Can I come over this weekend?"

"I really need to talk today."

She let out a deep sigh.

"Please, I don't know who else to talk to."

"Ok, fine. Is six ok?"

"Do you want to meet at The Lowry?"

"Sure," she replied as she hung up.

After our last encounter I had anticipated this conversation going much worse, and while she wasn't interested in talking on the phone, I hoped she would at least have the decency to reason with me in person.

11

The Lowry was nearly full. Generally, Linda and I would go there after therapy or in the morning, but never at 6:00 pm when the dinner rush was still going on. I put my name in at the hostess station and waited. They initially told me it would be twenty to thirty minutes, but it was getting close to the 45-minute mark, and Linda still hadn't arrived.

"Steve, party of two," the hostess announced.

I got up and made my way to the stand.

"Where's the other guest?" The hostess asked.

"I'm sorry, my wife is a little late. She should be here any second." The term 'wife' always sounds better than 'soon to be ex-wife.'

"You should really have both guests present before you check in," the hostess said in that famous, passive-aggressive midwestern way. She grabbed a few menus and hastily walked me to a booth near the kitchen.

"Your server will be right with you."

I took a seat, so I could still see the front door.

"Hello!" A perky voice said. "I'm Maria, I'll be your server this evening. Is there something I can get for you to drink?"

"I'll just have a PBR tall boy, and a half a dozen oysters please."

"You got it! Are you waiting for someone?"

"Yes, my wife."

"Ok, well I'll keep an eye on the table. When she arrives, I'll try and get her order as soon as she shows up."

"Thank you," I replied.

Then Maria walked into the kitchen, and I sat there at the table waiting. Broaching this subject was going to be difficult, but it was the only way I could get Jackson the medicine he needed. We had to have a real talk about everything, and lay it out on the table so we could try and figure out our next moves. After all, Linda is the one who brought Jackson home, so she needed to be somewhat responsible for him.

Maria came back to the table with my beer and six oysters. "You need anything else?" She asked.

"This is good for now."

She nodded, still smiling, and went off to tend to her other tables as I poured lemon on the oysters. Minnesota isn't known for its fresh seafood, but that doesn't stop restaurants from trying to sell it. Even if they occasionally cause hepatitis if eaten raw, they are worth the gamble.

I slurped the first one out of its shell and washed it down with my beer. The door to the restaurant swung open, and I shifted my attention toward it, expecting Linda, but just saw an elderly couple walking in. I took out my phone and started browsing the internet while I prepared the second oyster. Then the third. The sixth.

I thought of ways I could convince her to help me. I could offer more visits to see her dad. Or we could split the costs. Or I could guilt trip her with the fact that she was the one who made us adopt the cat in the first place. After more time elapsed, I ordered a new beer and another half dozen oysters. The front door kept swinging open, and people kept filing in. After a while, I stopped looking at the door. Ten minutes, turned to twenty and then an hour. Before I knew it, it was past 8:00, and the table was littered with empty beer cans and melting ice from the aluminum oyster trays they had been bringing out.

Maria stopped by the table, a look of concern growing on her face, "Is everything ok?" She asked. She wasn't smiling anymore.

"Yes. Can I have the check please?"

"I'm sorry," she said as she took my empty beer cans off the table.

"For what?" I asked.

She didn't answer. She just blushed as she walked off into the kitchen,.

12

I pulled out my keys to unlock my door, but the deadbolt didn't make any noise. I pushed the door open, and Linda was sitting on the couch drinking a glass of red wine. Jackson was lying in a box, looking at her and not breaking eye contact when I made my way into the room. He didn't seem happy or upset that she was there, he was just confused about who this person was and what they were doing in our home. Linda didn't even notice him. A wide grin was across her face as she looked at me.

"Why are you here?" I asked.

"You said you wanted to meet, so here I am." She shrugged her shoulders full of confidence as the smile moved even further up her cheeks.

"Yeah. At The Lowry. Over two hours ago," I replied.

"It's awfully rude to keep someone waiting, isn't it?"

"Linda, what's going on here?"

She let out a short, small chuckle and stood up while finishing her glass of wine. She sauntered to the kitchen, and I could hear the glugging of a bottle and a hearty but happy sigh. Then she walked back into the room and sat down clumsily. She took another sip, closing her eyes and monotonically humming to herself, savoring the flavor. All this, while I stood in the doorway, waiting for some kind of explanation.

"Steve, everyone told me you were spiraling out of control and that I shouldn't even waste my time with you anymore. People said you weren't the same person and that I should go and find someone new because chances were, you were doing the same. For a long time I didn't want to believe them, but finally, I figured that there must be some truth to it. After all, you had spent time in Florida, and now you're working who knows where to support the drinking habit you have clearly picked up." She motioned to the dozens of beer bottles and cans that were lying all over the living room. "You were a lost cause. A ship set adrift. Then all of a sudden I get a call from you earlier today about meeting up at our old stomping grounds and honestly, Steven, at this point, it's just pathetic because I have moved on too."

A silence fell over the two of us. Linda seemed to be reveling in the moment, and I was still trying to piece together what exactly she was talking about. Linda looked at me surprised and then belted out forced, unnatural laughter.

"You haven't heard, Steven? I'm seeing someone else. That's why I was late tonight, and that's why I was sleeping in earlier this afternoon. You took too long Steven. Now this ship has sailed. That means no more easy street. No more advancing up the corporate ladder to high paying jobs you don't deserve. Most importantly, no more me."

Jackson got up and started to make a break for the open front door, which I had just realized was still ajar behind me. I stepped fully into my apartment and closed it. He continued to run toward me and rub on my leg. I picked him up, walked over to the couch, and sat down next to Linda, who was still gloating that she wasn't going to take me back. Jackson curled into a ball on my legs.

"Linda, I didn't call to get back together with you."

She let out another fake laugh and rolled her eyes. She paused briefly, breaking eye contact and then took a sizable gulp of red wine. Jackson was purring softly as I pet him in my lap.

"If that's the case," Linda said after a few brief moments of silence, "why would you call me to meet up again?"

"Jackson is sick," I said. "He's having seizures, and I can't afford the medicine without your help."

"This is why you called me down here?" She said, her tone changing from one of piousness to anger, "You want me to give you money for your stupid cat?"

"Do I need to remind you that you adopted him? You brought him into this house, and now he is sick. Without his medicine, he could die."

"Well, how much is it?" She said nearly slamming her wine glass onto the coffee table.

"The tests he needed and the medication were nearly $800. The medicine is about $300 every month and a half or so."

"What the fuck, Steve?! I'm not helping you pay for that!"

"Why not?" Jackson's eyes widened, and he got out of my lap and scampered into the kitchen.

"Because he's not my cat."

"You brought him here, you have a responsibili-"

"Do not play that card, Steven. You had responsibilities and commitments too. The only thing you care about is yourself and how this medicine is going to eat into your beer money."

"Linda, I don't want to spend the night playing the blame game, but you're the one who adopted this cat, and you are the one who walked out on me. Just because everyone is saying I'm wrong for not wanting my old life back doesn't make them right. I have been saying the same thing over and over for months, and I don't understand how you don't get this. I don't want to work under your dad, I don't want to have expectations pushed on me, and I don't want to spend my life with you. It's not your fault. It isn't any person's fault."

"I came here wanting to figure things out, Steven."

"If that were the case, you would have shown up to The Lowry. You wouldn't have broken into our home, drunk, to make some sort of weird point. You wouldn't have told me you have a new fling. If you want to figure things out then why are you playing these mind games?"

"Steven," she said, eyes tearing up, "I just want things to go back." She was crying now. Openly weeping as tears fell down her cheeks and splashed on her dress. We both knew where the conversation was going.

"Things can't go back, Linda."

Linda abruptly stood up, wiped her tears from her eyes and headed toward the door. She stood with her hand on the doorknob for a second and then turned around and looked at me. She wasn't angry, her face wasn't contorted into a condescending expression. It was just empty.

"I'm not giving you anything for that cat," she said sternly, and opened up the door. She quietly walked out into the icy evening. A small gust of wind made its way into the room before she slammed the door behind her. I sat there until her high heels popping against the sidewalk were low, dull scrapes in the distance. It reminded me of leaving Nikki's room in Florida, when I saw curtains hit the wine glass off her table and the pop as it shattered and swishing of wasted wine went all over the tile floor.

Jackson started walking toward me from the kitchen. He let out a soft meow and stretched his legs. He looked up at me and started purring loudly.

"We'll figure it out, bud," I said unconvincingly.

He didn't seem bothered though. He just rubbed on my legs and kept purring as I looked out the windows and thought about the last time I had opened them. I took out my phone and texted my old college roommates, Tim and Jeff. I generally would grab a beer with John, but we still weren't on speaking terms, and after the night I just had, I didn't want to be alone.

13

Liquor Lyles was the kind of bar we'd meet at in college, so it seemed like the kind of place we should do our reunion at. Cheap alcohol, lousy bar food, and pool were all we really needed to have fun. No intense guys, or loud drunk girls; just people drinking, which is precisely what you're supposed to do in a bar.

I walked through the doors and saw the place was full of empty booths and stools. There were easily less than ten people through the entire bar, and a majority of those people we over the age of fifty. Besides a couple in the far corner quietly talking to one another, everyone was alone. I showed the bouncer my ID and took a booth far away from everyone else.

I looked around to see a litany of confusing and mismatched decor plastered all over the walls. There were your standard beer advertisements, mirrors, and NFL signs, but there were also incompatible and outdated holiday decorations everywhere. There was a Santa in one part of the room, and fake cobwebs hung up in another. Underneath the bar were cheap red, white, and blue banners, and just above the jukebox was a green leprechaun's hat.

"What do you want?" A scratchy voice said next to me. I looked up to see a woman who was probably fifty but looked seventy standing there. She had sunken eyes, and deep wrinkles outlined her seemingly permanent scowl.

"Is anything on special?" I kindly asked.

"Everything's on special, son. That's the only way we get people in here."

"In that case, I'll have a Todd the Axeman."

"Hmmm." She then walked away.

I looked down at my watch, and realized it was 10:17, and any second now Jeff and Tim would be arriving. I figured neither would ever leave the Twin Cities because both were born and raised here, which was good because I was losing people to hang out with. As much as I loved Jackson, it wasn't enough to just have a one-way conversation with a cat.

The waitress briskly walked over and slammed down a foamy beer. She looked at me, with the same disapproving, sad, hollow eyes as before.

"Five dollars," she roared.

I reached into my wallet and gave her my card, but she shook her head.

"We don't take cards anymore."

"Oh, ok, well then I would like to start a tab."

"No tabs either. Pay per drink."

"Why?" I asked

"Why what?"

"Why would you do any of that?"

"Just the rules," she replied, shrugging her shoulders.

"Is there an ATM here?" I asked.

She motioned toward the back poolroom, and I stood up and made my way there. Without checking my balance, I took out $200 and sat back down. Just so it was visible, I fanned out the money and gave her a twenty.

"Now, I will hold this, and you can have a tab," she said. She didn't change her facial expression, and she turned around to walk away.

"Did you do that because you thought I wasn't going to pay?" I blurted out as she was just a few paces away from the table.

"Nothing personal, sweetie. You look rough."

Just then, I saw Tim walk in, and after handing his ID to the bouncer, he looked over the room. The once, drunk, shaggy roommate was replaced with a slender, well-groomed man. He wore a blue suit and boasted a red power tie. He looked like the guys we used to relentlessly make fun of in college. He nearly walked by my booth, and I grabbed his arm. He looked down, surprised, and then after a few seconds, I saw the pieces fall into place.

"Jesus, Steve?" He nearly yelled, "What the hell, man?" He was happy to see me, but through the happiness, I could sense the surprise. We hugged, and then we sat down opposite each other.

"What happened, Tim? I thought we were never gonna sell out?" I said, pointing at his suit.

"Yeah, I know, right? I got a job at a for-profit university after I graduated and worked my way up. It's a great job man! Pay is good, I get to travel a lot and meet a lot of cool people."

"Is the job itself ok?" I asked.

"It's fine. It's a job you know? A lot of meetings and shit, but it pays the bills."

"What'll you have?" The waitress croaked at Tim.

"Just water is fine."

She rolled her eyes and left.

"Water?" I asked.

"Yeah, man. I'm sober. I've been sober for over three years now. Ever since I met my wife, and she showed me how much I was drinking and how inappropriate I was behaving. After that it was easy to stop. Honestly, man, I haven't ever felt better."

"Oh," I said, sipping my drink.

"You should really consider it."

"No thanks," I quickly responded.

A few awkward seconds passed as we didn't make eye contact, and neither knew what to say.

"Hey, man," I exclaimed, "I never met your wife, what's she like?"

"She's great!" Tim smiled and pulled out his phone, frantically unlocking it and swiping through the pictures. "I know that it might sound cliché, but I don't know what I would do without her." The smile continued to creep up his face as he showed me the pictures of him and his wife snowboarding, then mountain climbing, then kayaking, and finally, tailgating at a football game with visible bottles of water in their hands.

"That's great. I'm glad the both of you are doing well. What does she do?"

"Well, she's still trying to figure that out. She has worked a few different jobs, but she just can't seem to find that niche that'll make her happy."

"Oh, so she just works some office job then?"

"No, she is staying at home now."

"I didn't know you had kids, show me some pictures of them."

"No, she is just at home." The smile drained from his face, and that uncomfortable air washed over the both of us again, and we sat there still for a more extended period of time in silence.

"What's up, boys?" We heard next to the table, and both of us shifted our attention to see a man with a long beard, bald head, and stout frame. Had I not known he was coming, I would have never guessed it was Jeff. He looked like he had some hard living post-college. His face was aged well beyond either Tim or myself. It was marred with acne nobody over the age of seventeen should have, and his teeth were yellowed. For Jeff, the party had never ended, and it showed.

Jeff sat down opposite of me, not leaving a lot of space for Tim, and he moved closer to the wall so Jeff's body fat wouldn't be rolling on top of him. He was breathing heavily, and getting to Liquor Lyles had significantly taxed him.

"So, Jeff," I started, "what do you do now?"

Jeff laughed for a few seconds about something. Tim and I shot confused glances at one another, and after a while, he said, "Well, what I do isn't exactly the kind of thing you want to talk about."

"So, it's illegal?" Tim asked judgmentally.

"Not exactly, but I wouldn't say it is legal either."

"Can you at least give us a hint?" I asked, intrigued.

Jeff looked around the bar cautiously. I'm sure he knew that it was empty all around us, but I assumed he was just making sure. Then, he leaned into the middle of the group and whispered nearly inaudibly, "I deal with cryptocurrencies."

"That's not illegal," Tim groaned.

"How we get them is. That's all I have to say."

"What'll you have?" The waitress suddenly said. All of us jolted up because none of us heard or saw her coming.

"I'll have a Jack on the rocks." Jeff said as the waitress put down Tim's drink.

"What the fuck is that? Straight vodka?"

"It's water," Tim cooly said.

"Can you not afford a drink?" Jeff asked.

"I can afford a drink."

"Then what the hell?"

"He's sober now, Jeff," I said, wanting this moment to be over.

"You're shitting me." Jeff yelled, shocked. "You're going to tell me, Tim, no wait, sorry, 'Any-Time-Tim' doesn't drink anymore?"

"Yes." Tim said, his anger barely even being concealed anymore.

"Why?"

"Well, my wife-"

"Oh, don't give me that shit, Tim! You're better than that. Ever since you met this lady, you've been a ghost." Jeff turned his attention to me, "Same goes for you, Harding. Ever since you met Linda back in college, you vanished. Just because the two of you got some pussy, you think your friends don't mean shit anymore."

"No, Jeff. You just don't mean shit anymore," Tim snapped.

"Then why would you even agree to come to this? What was the point of meeting up with a loser like me? I'm sure getting a text from Steve an hour ago disrupted your perfect evening you had planned with your wife you can't leave for ten minutes."

"Because you prick, Steve is going through a divorce."

Jeff stopped yelling, and Tim immediately buried his head into his hands, embarrassed about what he had blurted out. He always had a bit of a temper, but the booze used to smooth that out. Now, with only a wife and no alcohol, and no real outlet, Tim couldn't hold back.

"Is that true, Harding?" Jeff solemnly said.

"Yeah, it's true."

"What exactly happened?" Tim asked.

"I don't know. I think it was a lot of different things. Now, there's no going back. We can't fix it."

"You can if you really want it," Tim said, enthusiastically.

"Even if I really wanted it, no we couldn't."

Everyone looked around the table, not sure what we should do next. I had about half my beer, and I quickly drank it all and caught the attention of our waitress as I tapped on the glass, showing I wanted another.

"That's not true," Tim indignantly replied. "You can fix this!"

"It doesn't seem like he wants to," Jeff uttered.

"Of course he does. He got married. Nobody gets married to get divorced."

We all sat there uncomfortably, not sure how any of us could progress the conversation and not cause an argument.

"You remember back in the day when we used to banter and mess with each other? Back before the mortgages, and the fake social media friends, the marriages, and the bullshit? What happened to that? How has this changed so much?"

The waitress came by and put my beer down on the table and left, not wanting to ask if anyone needed anything else. Sad people were good for business and interrupting a touching moment meant she could lose out on tips later.

"Is there anything I can do to help?" Tim sheepishly asked.

"No, Tim. Nobody can do anything."

"Well, I don't believe that," Tim said, nudging Jeff out of the booth. "And if you change your mind, you can call me up again, but if it's going to be this same old story, I don't want to hear it." He was out of the booth and put on his jacket, now looking down at both Jeff and me, "Take care, the both of you." Then he left, full of conviction and pride.

Jeff and I were alone, and across from each other. He made a face making fun of Tim's stiffness and newfound hope in sobriety. A snooty, 'I'm too good for this,' kind of mocking and it made both of us laugh.

"You ever think he'd turn out like that?" Jeff asked.

"I didn't think any of us would turn out like this."

"What else could there be? A married, successful guy, who's sober and boring, a struggling divorced guy, and me. That's kind of all there is. Don't get me wrong, it's a spectrum, but what else can you be after college? An artist? Man, the only artist any of us know is Jason, and he can only afford to do political art in San Francisco because of his parents. An actor? Everyone makes fun of drama kids at every grade in school. Or a scientist doing research? I don't know one person trying to cure cancer. How is that possible?"

"Maybe we just hung out with the wrong people."

"Or, maybe, none of this shit matters."

"Regardless of what we turned out to be, I'm glad we aren't Tim," I said.

We both laughed, and Jeff finished his drink, and held it up, ordering another.

"Can I ask you something?" Jeff asked, spitting ice back into his glass.

"Sure."

"Why did you want us all to meet tonight? I haven't seen you since college, and I heard from you sparingly after you met Linda too. I'm sure it was the same for Tim. Why now? Why try and get us all together?"

"You know, I thought it was because I was lonely, but now I'm not sure."

"What do you mean?"

"You both have Facebook. I occasionally look and see what you two have been doing. I deep down knew that tonight was going to be as messy as it was. I knew Tim was religious now. All of his posts are about Jesus and rebirth. I saw your drunk party pictures as well. I mean, tonight was not going to not be a repeat of college, I think we all knew that."

"Then, why did you ask us to meet?"

"For once, I just wanted something to be as good as I remembered it."

For a while we talked about the glory days. We reminisced about girls we had slept with, and pranks we pulled for an hour or two, then we parted ways. We all left that night, and all of us felt sorry for the others. Still, I'm sure none of us felt good.

14

Bill looked at me suspiciously. I knew he could see the dark rings under my eyes. I also knew he could smell the faint aroma of last night's beers slowly making their way out of my pores. Regardless, it was 6:30 in the morning, right when my shift was supposed to start, and there I was.

"Are you going to show up hungover every day?" He asked.

"Give or take," I replied.

"Well, honestly, as long as you're here and functional I really don't care. Usually, the college kids won't show up after a night of boozing."

"Bill, I'm going to need some extra shifts."

"They certainly don't ask for that either."

"I'm serious man, my cat-"

"Oh, you actually have a cat? I thought you made that up to go drinking with your buddies last night."

"No, man. My cat had a seizure, and yesterday I had to take him to the vet. Then I had to meet with my ex-wife to see if she could help me out with the medication cost. After that I went out drinking."

"I'm sure that was a fun meeting," Bill scoffed sarcastically. "I remember when my first wife and I got divorced. I wasn't making much, but she still stopped by and tried to get more money from me."

"For what?"

"I can't remember. Some utility bill, or rent, or car note. Who cares?"

"What happened?"

"Probably the same thing that happened with you and your ex last night."

The door's motion sensor rang, and a disheveled middle-aged man shuffled in and made his way to the coffee. Bill gently put his hand on my shoulder and nodded sympathetically at me. "I'll see what I can do about those extra hours." He said and walked toward the back of the convenience store where his office was. There wasn't anything particularly good or bad about Bill. He seemed like a typical forty something dad. Still, he was one of the best bosses I've ever had.

The middle-aged man came to the counter with his coffee. He set it down in front of me and stared, patting his jeans, searching for his wallet. This turned into him frantically patting his pockets again, and then an embarrassed look flashed over his face.

"Just take it," I said.

He didn't say anything. He just smiled, and nodded and made his way out of the store. Super America could afford to take the .95 cent hit. Other employees unofficially recommended I do this occasionally to build a rapport with repeat customers. The cheap offering would make that man more inclined to come back, and in turn, make the company even more money. Also, I was too tired from drinking last night to care enough for a fellow borderline alcoholic to be forced to rummage through the change in his car so he could buy something we essentially make for free.

I would consider this a win-win.

15

I cracked open a beer when I got home to celebrate the fact that I left work with a string of new shifts Bill had given me. They were shitty hours, and some of them meant that I would have to pull doubles, but they would at least be a step in the right direction so I could start saving the money for Jackson's medicine.

I sat down on the couch, but I was followed to it by a hungry and meowing cat. Jackson jumped up next to me and started purring as he sat on my lap and curled up into a ball. I began to pet him, and he was just about to fall asleep when my phone rang and vibrated in my pocket, making him alert, and he dashed away.

I fished the phone out of the front of my pants and looked at the screen. It was Linda. There was a picture of her from a day we were walking downtown, and it started raining, so she stole a giant black trash bag from a custodian's cart and carved a hole into it. It was a bizarre and silly picture, and even though I was never excited to hear from her, I had forgotten all about that photo.

"Linda?" I asked.

"What are you doing right now, Steve?" She asked.

"Just at home, relaxing. Why?"

"I might have to cash in that offer from a few meetings ago."

"What?"

"I need you to come with me to see Dad."

"When?"

"Now."

"Well, what time?"

"Like, ten minutes. We need to get to the doctor."

"Well, shit, are you going to pick me up?"

"Yeah. I'll be there soon."

Then she hung up.

16

Linda was in the parking lot in ten minutes, just like she said on the phone. It was enough time for me to finish my beer and be buzzed so I could deal with a family I was sure didn't want to see me. I opened the car and got in the passenger seat, and immediately, Linda asked, "Have you been drinking?"

"No."

"Well, you smell like it."

"Yeah, some of the beer in the cooler was dropped on the ground and exploded on me at work today. You gave me less than ten minutes from when I got home to get in this car. So, here I am. Do you want me to shower?"

She didn't answer, she already was pulling out of the parking lot halfway through my bullshit excuse. Her eyes were fixated on the car in front of us, and a look of panic was in her eyes. Linda lost her cool around me sometimes, but they were always situations that were more heat of the moment. We would be arguing, and she would lose her grip on that stability she had, and would lash out. It was definitely happening more post-divorce than ever before. Still, when she got upset and even when she started yelling it was short lived. Her face would go back to that collected, calm expression she always had on.

Right now though, she had a wild look in her eyes. She was confused, and the even-keeled nature that she usually had was draining from her every second. I didn't know the specifics of how her dad was doing, but it had to be something significant. To pick me up after the argument last night, to call in my one time agreed upon visit, to be this chaotic and panicked, to not have me take a shower even though I smelled like a brewery, something had gone wrong.

"You want to tell me what's happening?" I asked.

"Dad is having chemotherapy today," She sullenly said.

"Don't they schedule those weeks in advance?"

"Yes."

"Then why did you pick me up in such a hurry? You could have let me know earlier."

"Because Sasha is going to be there."

"I thought Sasha lived in Chicago."

"She does, but she thought it would be good to see Dad for this treatment."

"So, you are making me go to your dad's chemotherapy appointment because your sister is in town?"

"She doesn't know about us yet," Linda said, eyes not breaking with the car in front of her.

"Yeah, I severely doubt that."

"Steve. This really isn't the time."

"Hey, it was your pick of whenever you wanted. If it is because of a sibling rivalry thing, I really don't care."

"This is why we're separated, Steve," Linda snapped. "Because you're such an asshole."

I was going to retort, but what's the point? I either could prove her point and make a comment, or stay quiet and feel better about myself.

17

Linda didn't say anything for the rest of the drive. When she parked the car in the big, empty lot, I noticed we were in front of a nameless and anonymous building. It seemed like a bleak place to receive the last treatments of someone's life. It wasn't inappropriate, it was just grey and unassuming. Like a vacuum cleaner outlet store, or an attorney's office who specializes in DUI cases.

Without saying another word, Linda led the way, through the front doors and to the left down a long, seemingly endless, hallway.

"This is where Dad has been getting his treatments." She nearly whispered as we walked deeper and deeper into the endless maze of corridors and lobbies.

"Hey, what should I call your dad?" I asked.

She shot me a confused glance.

"You know, as a joke, I used to call him Pop, but now I think that's inappropriate?"

"Just call him Greg."

We walked for another thirty feet until Linda stopped in front of a door. It didn't have anything on it, just the number 194 next to it.

"Ok," Linda said calmly, "this place is always calm and sad, so please just try and be quiet and respectful in there."

"Yeah, I get it, Linda," I said.

"I'm just saying I can't take anymore embarrassment from-"

"Jesus Christ, Linda. I get it."

She opened the door, and initially, I heard nothing. I braced myself for what I was sure was going to be an intense few hours, and I started to feel the buzz from the beer instantly vanish.

We walked into the room, and there were over a dozen large, leather chairs lining the wall, ready for people to sit in and take their medicine. There was only a small, elderly woman wrapped in quilts sitting by herself, and a cluster of people in the far right corner of the room. Through the group, I could see Greg, and I recognized Sasha even though I hadn't seen her since the wedding. I also noticed Linda's mom, Martha, in the crowd, sitting right across from Greg, soothingly stroking his outstretched arm.

As we approached, I could tell something was wrong. Not wrong in the sense of an emergency, just somewhat amiss. People looked confused, and Greg's face was tomato red as he seethed in the chair. It was a face I had come to recognize from Linda from our separation process.

"Hey everyone!" Linda announced as we neared the mass of people. "What's wrong?"

"They won't give me the goddamn treatment," Greg mumbled under his breath.

"Why not?" Linda asked.

"Because," a calm voice said from behind us, "his blood pressure is unreasonably high. Greg needs to get to a hospital right away to bring down his numbers before we can administer anything."

"It's fine the way it is," Greg blurted out.

"No, it certainly is not. Your numbers of 223/156 are so dangerous you could have a stroke at any moment. On top of that, you want to administer chemotherapy? Not a chance."

"What if I sign something, and decide to take the risk on my own?" Greg asked.

"Absolutely not."

"Listen here, my daughter came here from Chicago to go through this with me. I need this done tonight."

"No, you don't," Sasha said. "Listen to the doctor and stop arguing. We're going to the hospital."

"I don't want to go to the goddamn hospital!" He yelled.

"Keep your voice down," Martha whispered as her face blushed.

"It doesn't matter what you want, Dad. You're going."

Greg's eyes darted around at each of the family members, hoping someone would save him, but everyone just avoided eye contact. Everyone except me. When his eyes met mine, he scoffed and said, "What is he doing here? You're too good to come to work, too good for my daughter, but you're not too good to come see an old man die?"

"Linda asked me to come, Greg."

"I'm your boss!" He yelled, "You'll address me the way you address a boss, you are to call me Mr.-"

"Well, I don't work there anymore do I?"

His face continued to redden, and he sighed, infuriated by what I had said.

"That doesn't matter though does it now, Greg. Don't bring that blood pressure up more. Let's get you to the hospital, so you don't have a stroke." Martha said trying to diffuse the situation.

"You," he said defiantly as he pointed at me, "aren't going to do shit."

"Fine with me."

Greg got up, waving off help and made his way to the door with Martha. Slowly, a few family members followed behind him to make sure the hospital would be able to bring down his obscenely high blood pressure. At that moment, I felt bad for him. Sure, he was a dick, and yeah, he had this uncanny ability to turn people off from him immediately, but he was still a man. A man who had worked hard his whole life and had taken control of his own destiny. Someone who refused to say no, played by the rules, and had become a successful company man. But even if you take control of your life, you can't control sickness, and you can't control death. Now, both were confronting him, and he couldn't do anything about it.

"Thanks," Sasha said to me.

"I can't tell if you're being sarcastic or not."

"I'm not. We've been trying to get him to go to the hospital for forty-five minutes, and he has just been yelling at everyone. You must have broken him somehow."

"Well, I don't think he ever liked me that much."

"Don't take it personally. He never really liked anyone."

"Can you two not talk about Dad like that?" Linda interjected.

"He's my dad too," Sasha said. "And for the moment, he is still Steve's as well."

"What do you mean 'for the moment'?" Linda asked, her voice filled with confrontational angst.

Sasha rolled her eyes and stared at Linda. It was a look siblings give each other when one of them is badly lying. "Even if I hadn't just heard what Dad said, I still have family and friends in Minneapolis that tell me what's going on."

"Well, nothing is going on," Linda snapped.

"Ok," Sasha said, moving her ruby red hair from her face. "If that's the case, want to go grab dinner with me?"

"That sounds great," Linda replied in a snarky tone.

"Uh, Linda. I have to work tomorrow morning," I said.

"We can make some time," she answered for me.

"Great. Where do you two want to go?" Sasha asked.

I already knew before Linda replied.

"The Lowry."

18

Sasha was different than the last time I had seen her years ago. Before she moved to Chicago, she had looked almost identical to Linda, but now you could hardly tell they were sisters. Her hair was a deep, fake shade of red, and a few tattoos showed on her forearm. Her clothes were black with no visible brand, and it all made her light blue eyes shine through her bangs that much more. She was like a real, more punk version of Jessica Rabbit from *Who Framed Roger Rabbit*.

"What can I get for you three?" The waitress suddenly said.

"I'll have a PBR and a dozen oysters," I blurted out.

"Again?" She said laughing, "Don't you ever get tired of those?" She nudged my arm jokingly and I realized it was the waitress from the previous night when Linda had stood me up.

"You mind if I have a few of those oysters?" Sasha asked.

I shook my head.

"In that case, I will have a few of his oysters and your tomato soup with the grilled cheese."

"I'll have," Linda started without waiting, "the turkey burger."

"Great! The oysters will be right out, and then I'll bring out the rest of your order when it's ready."

She winked at me and went back into the kitchen.

"You know her?" Sasha asked.

"Nope."

"Then why is she so flirty with you?"

"Couldn't tell you."

"I have to use the bathroom," Linda said, and she got up and went toward the back of the restaurant. Once she had rounded the corner, Sasha quickly turned around in her seat and said, "Can you please tell me what is going on with you two?"

"Why don't you ask your sister?"

"Because she won't tell me. Nobody will tell me anything."

"I don't know if it's my place to say something then."

"She's my sister Steve. I do deserve to know."

"Fine, we're separated."

"Ok, how do things look regarding getting back together?"

"Not great."

"Why not? You find someone new?"

"It's not like that."

"Dude, someone does not leave a cush job, a hot wife, and an easy life for nothing. No bullshit. What's up?"

"She left me a while ago, and I can't really bring myself to put it back together."

"Why not?"

"Why?"

"Because you can have your old life back. She left you, and now I'm sure she's regretting it. Why not take advantage? Are you planning on getting a bunch of money out of the divorce? Do you want to just watch it burn? Do you want her to look like a fool? What is the point?"

"Sasha, I hate to disappoint you, but there isn't a massive cover-up going on here. I don't want to hurt her, and I don't want a bunch of money. I just don't want to go back. There's nothing there for me. I already know it was mediocre, so why would I fight to have it back and then fight to keep a marriage together I don't even want anymore?"

"So, seriously? You are just bailing?"

"Technically, she bailed."

"Fair."

The waitress came from the raw bar and put the metal tin of oysters in the middle of the table. She noticed the seriousness of the conversation, and briskly walked away. Sasha instantly grabbed one.

"You're going to have more than a few aren't you?" I asked.

"Yeah, probably." Sasha grinned.

Linda, appeared out of the back of the restaurant, sat down at the table, and settled into her chair.

"What were you two talking about?"

"Just some stuff about Dad." Sasha replied.

"What stuff?" Linda asked, clearly irritated and not believing her sister.

"Just stuff."

"Hey, I never asked, why are you named Sasha?" I asked as I slurped down one of the oysters.

"I'm not joking, you two," Linda replied, trying to wrestle control of the conversation out of our hands.

"Really, Linda," Sasha replied. "Nothing."

Linda looked at us suspiciously. She knew we were lying, but what could she possibly say? Sasha wasn't mad at me. Actually, she was indifferent about whatever we were discussing. With nothing else to talk about we all sat there for a while, silently eating oysters and drinking.

After some time had passed, Linda had mustered the strength to tactfully address us, and just as she was opening her mouth to ask us more questions, her phone rang. She grimaced, but she took the phone out of her purse and looked at Sasha.

"It's Dad," she said.

"Why don't you answer it?"

Linda was torn. She didn't want to leave us alone to continue our conversation, but she also didn't want to leave Greg alone after the nightmare at the chemotherapy treatment center.

"Fine, I'll be right back," she said before she got up and walked out of the restaurant.

Sasha took another oyster out of the tin.

"Do you want to go out too?"

"Not really. I already know what the conversation is going to be. He's going to yell about how he needs new doctors, we are going to argue they're the best in the city. He's going to say how he doesn't give a damn. He's so predictable that his words and actions are almost scripted." She dressed the oyster with cocktail sauce and horseradish as she spoke.

"You know, I'm almost sure your sister made me come to this today because you were here. I think she wanted to put on a show that we were still together."

"I figured. Linda is not like her father."

"What do you mean?"

"Well," Sasha said before taking down the oyster, "just like Dad prefers to lash out with anger when something he doesn't like happens, Linda tries to cover it up, but that's only for a while. That means if you two do end up getting a divorce, buckle up because it is going to be an arduous, uphill fight."

"If she wants everything to be covered up, why would she make it more difficult?"

"Once everyone knows, she will make herself look like she is the victim. Like she was wronged."

"Good to know."

"What I'm telling you is be careful. Even if you're sure this is the route you want to go, tread lightly. It might be advantageous to re-evaluate your situation."

"Why are you telling me all this?"

"I'm just trying to help my sister. The easier it is for her, the better for everyone."

Linda came back into the restaurant and sat down at our table. She looked frantically at the two of us. I could tell she wanted to ask what we were talking about again, but it would have seemed too desperate. There was also urgency in her eyes that eclipsed the need to join in our gossip.

"We need to get back to the chemo center. Dad got his blood pressure lowered at the hospital, and we can support him while he gets his treatment."

We all sat there, looking uncomfortably at one another.

"Linda," Sasha started, "there is no way they are going to administer chemotherapy just because his blood pressure was lowered with medicine less than twenty minutes ago. Even if they would, which they won't, the center has to be closed by now."

"Well, they'll let him in," she replied defiantly.

"I have to work tomorrow, Linda. I need to go home."

"Steven, I need you to come," Linda said, as she glared at me.

"Why?"

The question took her off guard. She sat there for a second, shocked by it, but even after that wore off, she continued to stare at me, dumbfounded and angry.

"Did you hear the way Greg spoke to me? Why would I go back?"

Sasha gave me a curious look.

"He was just mad at the doctors. He wasn't mad at you, Steve."

"Well, I'm not going. That was humiliating and disrespectful."

"Steven, can I talk with you outside?" Linda asked, agitated.

"No." I replied. I took out $60 and put it on the table.

Linda's stare intensified as I drank the last few gulps of my PBR.

Sasha, on the other hand, smiled at me.

With that, I walked out of The Lowry for the last time.

Troy Bernardo

GOODBYE

I remember that last night I saw Linda because it was so normal above anything else. I was at the gas station, working the counter. It was the graveyard shift, and I was only a few hours in at that point. The night had been mostly quiet. A few sixteen-year-olds buying condoms, some kids trying to buy beer and getting upset when I asked for their IDs.

At this point though, right before, during, and after bar close, you got all the desperate smokers and the people who had recently quit smoking, wander in to get a fresh pack. You rarely had any trouble and the most excitement you got out of an evening was a mentally ill bum coming in and yelling nonsense at everyone.

That night though, it was exceptionally slow. I sat at the counter, alone and bored out of my mind, thumbing through the magazines and going through my phone. I heard the bell ring and two figures step through the door. I quickly pretended like I was grabbing something from underneath the counter and when I looked up, I saw a large, in shape, tattooed man in a black tank top with Linda. The door was a little ways from me, but I heard her whisper something to him. Both of them looked in my direction and laughed as they walked toward me.

"I'll put forty on pump five and a pack of Camel Lights."

"No problem, man," I said, punching in the numbers on my register and grabbing a pack of cigarettes. "Anything else?" I asked.

"Nope," he said. But he didn't leave. He stared at me. Then he grabbed his cigarettes and started to pack them against his palm for a while until he felt like he had non-verbally threatened me enough.

"Have a nice night!" I said as he walked out of the store.

"Jealous?" Linda asked.

"Of what?"

Linda rolled her eyes and said, "You know of what."

"No, I really don't. That being said, I'm glad you're happy."

Linda stared at me for a while. She wanted me to say something, but I had no idea what.

"How's your dad?" I asked.

"What do you care?" She snapped. I knew how her dad was doing. Not well. But, I still thought it would be polite to ask.

We stood there, across from the stain smeared counter and looked around. Sometimes at each other, sometimes not, but for a long while, we were both just there in Super America, not sure what to do.

"Was it all worth it?" She suddenly said, breaking the silence, "Was this the life you wanted? Was this the life worth destroying our marriage for? Your career for? Your friendships? Your family? My family? Was it what you dreamed it would be, Steven?"

"It's not like that. I didn't leave you because you weren't good, and I didn't leave the job because it wasn't easy, my family hasn't essentially exiled me because they're bad people. This might not be the life I drew up when I was younger, but it certainly is better than the life I had before. Does that make sense?"

"No, Steven it doesn't. And, it never will."

Just then, her new boyfriend came through the door and yelled, "Let's go, babe! We have to get to Tofur's. He said to meet him after bar close." Then he vanished back outside and made his way toward the pumps, smoking his cigarette the whole way.

"You should get to Tofur's," I said.

She waited for one more second and stared at me. For the first time since I can remember, we were together, in that backyard of my college house, listening to the muffled sounds of a party inside and looking at each other. Both of us genuinely wondering what the other was thinking. Then, just like that, she turned around and walked out into the summer evening. Before getting in his car, her new boyfriend tried to eye me down through the window, but quickly recognized I wasn't interested in either of them. Then he got into his Dodge Charger and drove off.

Bill came out of his office and smiled at me. "I'm proud of you, Steve," he said. "You really were the bigger person there."

"Thanks, Bill," I said, beaming with pride.

"Hey, some drunk guy puked in the boy's bathroom a few hours ago, and it needs to get cleaned up."

Then, Bill went back to his office.

Once he left, I pretended like I was tying my shoes as I tucked a pack of Newports into my sock. Sometimes, on these hot summer nights, I like to act like I am back in Florida. I smoke Nikki's favorite brand and out behind the dumpster, I listen to the wind whip the leaves, and I imagine we're standing on the beach together and the tide is rolling in.

Troy Bernardo

ABOUT THE AUTHOR

Troy Bernardo is a high school English teacher. He completed his Master's in Communications Education in 2018 and currently resides in San Diego, California. Originally from Port Orange, Florida, Troy received his Bachelor's Degree from Florida International University. From there, he continued to travel for several years living and working in Alaska, South Korea, Minneapolis, and finally settling in California. Troy loves to cook, drink local beers, and spend time with his two cats, Jax and Maya, and his wife, Laura. *Hardly Harding* is Troy's first published work, but just one of many full-length novels he has written.